LOOK! LOOK! FEATHERS

STORIES BY
MIKE YOUNG

For Alina!
Arkansas snow
ridge/eyes & more!

Word Riot Press
Middletown, New Jersey
December 2010

xo,

Look! Look! Feathers by Mike Young
A Word Riot Press Book
Copyright 2010
ISBN: 978-0-9779343-6-2
LCCN: 2010935366

Many thanks to the following publications, where the following stories appear in earlier forms: *Monday Night* & *Hobart.com*: "The Peaches Are Cheap"; *Backwards City Review* & *Route 9*: "Burk's Nub"; *Washington Square Review*: "Look! Look! Feathers"; *Keyhole*: "The World Doesn't Smell Like You"; *The Collagist*: "What The Fuck Is An Electrolyte?"; *American Short Fiction*: "Snow You Know and Snow You Don't"; *Hobart #10*: "Stay Awhile If You Can"; *Juked.com*: "No Such Thing As a Wild Horse" (as "And the Shoes on the Cables Are There For the Angels")

Word Riot is a monthly online literary magazine dedicated to the forceful voices of up-and-coming writers. Word Riot Press is the print extension of the magazine, publishing chapbooks and paperbacks. For more information please contact us:

Word Riot/Word Riot Press
PO Box 414
Middletown, NJ 07748
www.wordriot.org
www.wordriot.org/press

Cover and book design by Bryan Coffelt
Book was typeset in Garamond
Printed in the U.S.A.

"Young hits the mark in this smart, quirky debut collection, where base humanity is juxtaposed against a crushing swell of technology and pop culture. Social media, brain-Internet browsers, and reality television all feature in Young's stories, and institutions like the 24-hour grocery, the 'old hotel on Mason Street,' and Facebook are venues for Young's twisted tales. This is a slick collection—relevant, wise, and immensely enjoyable."

— PUBLISHERS WEEKLY

"A fascinating book with lots of stuff in it, all the best stuff, funny stuff. Mike Young writes like the guy in the Viagra ad, the one whose erection is way past its four hours. He's headed for the emergency room now. Go with him. See what happens."

— FREDERICK BARTHELME, author of *Waveland*

CONTENTS

No one knows how to love anybody's trouble

—Frank Stanford

THE PEACHES ARE CHEAP

It's August, and it smells like grass and cranberry fruit snacks. I pick my brother up from the post office where he works. When he gets in, he says, "Let me take off these shoes."

We drive and see things: old fences, a barbecue in a motel courtyard.

"Are you guys semi or official or what?" I ask.

We see hobos in swimming trunks, chlorine hands, this boy with a mohawk playing the violin on a porch. Earlier this summer, my brother delivered a JCPenny catalog to the wrong apartment number. He met this woman there. She was spraying Raid around her windowsill. Now they fuck.

"It's something," my brother says. "It's not letting down."

"So why did she leave Eugene again?"

"I didn't tell you in the first place. This guy, this stalker guy, right? He breaks in and hangs out on her balcony? She finds him there, saying something. I forget what."

We see shirtless skateboarders, shoes tied to power lines, evening sunlight that falls like an arm across a pillow.

"That's sad," I say.

"It's creepy as shit."

I shrug. "What now?"

"I think I'll hit her with a pipe wrench."

We laugh. We see dust motes and Kool-Aid stains, sweat, our own thoughts of shower curtains and flesh.

There's a scab under my eye, so I scratch it.

"I want to turn into a firecracker," I say.

He spits. "I want to turn into a basketball star."

It's one of our tired little games.

"Let's learn to drive steamships," I say.

He kind of smiles.

We go to the supermarket and buy canned peaches. The cashier squints at my brother. He winks and steals a penny from the charity saucer. Out in the parking lot, we eat the peaches with our car doors open.

"I'll tell ya," my brother says, and he sighs.

We used to shove each other off of rope swings. We used to shove each other off of fire escapes. Now I work for the gas company. He works at the post office.

I nod.

Sometimes, under this drawl of light, a dying will find your jaw. There are old fences and old dogs all over this town. By September, my brother will be seeing the supermarket teller and scoring free beer.

I drop him off at his place. Before he leaves, he leans into my window for a long time, then he thanks me for the ride. I think to ask him about playing pool, about buying a pizza.

Instead, I say, "Tomorrow, right? Like Batman. Same time, same channel."

"No shit?" he says. He laughs and leaves, hands in his back pockets.

The sun hits him like a cigarette ad.

It's August, and it smells like wrenches, grass, distant water.

I drive home with my eyes open, then I drive with them closed, hoping to hit something, anything, like a refrigerator box, or a wall of lightning bugs, or a kid on his bicycle, the only thing he really loves.

BURK'S NUB

On Thursday, during lunch in the math teacher's room, Burk showed us the progress of his nub. It was growing on top of his hand. Filmy and slightly inflamed, it seemed covered in pork silk. Sure, it looked bigger and rounder. The lights inside it, tiny pinpoints, looked brighter. Even whirring a little, maybe.

We first saw it two weeks ago. I guess we all noticed it, but Ty was the first to say something. Ty plays trumpet in the school band and brags about drinking beer with his uncle. "What the fuck is that?" he asked. Burk wouldn't say how he got it, but he claimed the nub hooked him into the internet. Fuzzy web pages popped straight into his brain. He said he aced his last physics test by Googling the answers. After Burk showed us his test, Ty snorted. "If I brought home a fucking physics test like that," he said, "my parents would *fork* over the dough." Burk squeezed his nub and nodded.

At lunch, Ty shrugged. "Scary shit. But whatever." He shotgunned a bottle of Cherry Coke then reached into his bag for the next one. We all backed away from Burk, mulling above our chairs before sitting— disappointed spectators post-spectacle. Burk sagged and folded his hands in his lap. He watched us and chortled, a glugging sort of sound.

Burk plays tuba, usually tries to hide behind it, but you can't miss him. His thighs are Christmas hams. People call him Jabba the Hutt, and he's aware of this. He wears only two or three stretched and torn T-shirts, all of them navy school shirts. Sometimes he wears his P.E. shirt, which is pathetic. But when you don't have the money for a lousy Metallica t-shirt, what do you do? At home, they say, he goes shirtless. That's something I don't think about.

Ty is thick and puffy, but not so hippoesque as Burk. He can carry himself out of that band room with a clipped strut, something the rest of us can't manage. I mean, he still plays Magic—greasy face, never gets laid—but he owns this heat. Say two of us band kids are at our stands, mumbling back and forth, and Ty sits between us. He'll snap open his trumpet case and we'll turn to face the front. He might get to play trumpet onstage as a Roman in the spring musical, that one about the forum.

I know the Romans or the Greeks or something used to take baths with little boys, but I don't know if they had trumpets or tubas. Burk plays his tuba in the back by the instrument lockers. He could tell me about the Romans, hit up the ol' Wikipedia. We talk to him more since the nub. We didn't talk to him much before, and he would eat grilled cheese sandwiches by himself. One time a choirgirl turned to him and said, "I've never seen you without a grilled cheese sandwich." After she said this, his eyes went small. I remember that his pupils looked like tiny sailboats, those boats you can barely see from the beach.

❧

On Thursday, we had lunch. Lunch meant playing cards and arguing about the differences in D&D and Japanese-style RPGs, listening without admitting it for the polo shirts and miniskirts to laugh down the hall, back from the fast food places. After lunch, some of us trudged over to Advanced Band. It was hot, and Burk seemed to sweat more than usual. I mean, I wasn't measuring it in a test tube or anything, but he was having trouble, missing notes, and I kept glancing back at him. He was struggling. Shifting his hands all the time, like maybe the nub was bothering him. Ty shimmied as he played, grooved like a dork, but hey, that's Ty. As usual, he was a little sharp on everything. Our conductor, Mr. Slocum—who has bald eyebrows and Snowman Slocum for a nickname—kept pinching his nose and whining about both of them. We were in a sour mood when the bell rang.

Ty's not normally a violent dude, just sort of a smart-ass, so when he slapped Burk in the head, that was weird. We were in physics, and Mr. Hogan asked about some constant. Ty started rifling through the book, but Burk said the whole damn thing in a split second. Ten digits long and he spat it out. Then he sat back, wearing this sly little grin, really tickled. To be honest, I don't see Burk smile much. Then Ty had to hit him and call attention to our whole corner. I mean, I felt bad for Burk, but I felt bad for the clan. Us band geeks. Decked out in button-down shirts with dragons or black Pac-Man T-shirts, gangly and slouching, hoarding the dignity of silence. Then Ty has to go break all that because he's pissed. To be honest, you won't see any of us smile much.

After school, I walked to the dirt lot behind the gym where most kids parked. The ones without the cute Volkswagens and waxed Jeeps, anyway. I walked with Ty, who was still fuming. I caught my reflection in his windshield. Four new pimples. I grimaced and leaned in closer. "What, you want to steal my car?" Ty asked.

"I was counting how many bugs you kill," I said.

"Your mom's a bug," Ty said.

I squinted at the sun and thought of the afternoon ahead: bouncing between television and message boards, shoveling Doritos.

"Can I get a ride?" I asked.

"I'm late for something," Ty said, and climbed in before I could ask what he was late for. But I knew the answer as he drove off, slow because it was his grandma's car. You'd think with all his sharp notes and scowls he'd be roaring off somewhere, maybe getting a blowjob while he drove. But his answer was nothing. He was late for nothing. I enjoyed this until it made me feel dumb.

Then I started walking. After a couple blocks, I saw Burk. He walks home across the street from me. Turns left into the parking lot of these old yellow apartments, and I keep going. Sometimes we nod.

But this time Burk stopped and sat on the curb. So I crossed the street. When I reached him, I lagged, looking down, scratching my ear. I glanced over at the nub. Burk heaved himself up and we shuffled in step.

"It smells like the back of a Taco Bell," I said.

"You know how they do that?" Burk said. "They point their kitchen fans at the street. So you smell it."

I shrugged. "It's hot as hell."

We walked in silence, side-by-side, until he hit his turnoff. He headed into the parking lot, so I tossed him a nod and began to walk away. At the crosswalk, I heard him calling my name. I turned around. He was running to catch up, waddling really, and I had to put my fist over my mouth to keep from snorting because he looked like one of those strong men who drag airplanes with their shoulders.

He panted a second. "You want to hang? I mean, it's fine if you don't. It's just kind of hot, you know? My aunt's here. She has a car. Maybe she can give you a ride home?"

I would've said no, but his eyes started to shrink and bob around, and I remembered the sailboats. So I blew a breath and gave in, mumbling, "Sure, cool, whatever."

I followed him into his parking lot. His apartment complex was short and squat, yellow as fake cheese. Doors and windows spaced in uniform. It looked like a row of cubbyholes, the pattern only broken by things beside the doors: someone's pink stroller, a black trash bag.

Inside, it stank. As soon as it hit me, I tried not to notice. Actually, first I tried not to breathe, and then I tried not to notice. Old carpet, sweat, and roach spray all congealed into this weird, moist odor. Sure enough, Burk tossed his backpack and swiped off his shirt. He chucked it into a pile of similar shirts beside a television. His gut jiggled as he walked down a hallway. My imagination crossed its arms and nodded: yep, Jabba the Hut. I felt like a bastard.

I followed him. No one seemed to be there. I saw a kitchen of stains and dirty dishes, and I kicked a GI Joe out of my way.

"Where's your aunt?" I asked.

"Oh," Burk said. "I thought she was here." He turned into his room.

His room was chaos like the rest of the house—balled up socks and empty soda bottles. I was a little disappointed in his desk, though. Band geeks should have dignity in silence and dignity in beautiful desks. But his computer looked dusty, his monitor all small and dim. Game boxes and old joysticks were cluttered around his keyboard, really old joysticks. To be honest, I didn't see anything newer than the joysticks.

"You can sit down on the bed," he said. He booted up his computer and I watched him dial and squeal onto the internet. Dial-up. No shit.

"You still use it?" I asked. "Your computer, I mean. Even with the nub and everything?"

"Yeah. The nub still has a ways to go. It's kind of dim still."

"That sucks. Are you on a plan? Do you get like a pamphlet?"

"It doesn't work that way. It's from Japan. You get this—well, I can't really say. There's this non-disclosure thing. You put it in with this needle. I'm not a big fan of needles." He pointed at his bed. "I laid down, right? My aunt sort of did it for me. You have to rinse it too. Have you ever had your ears cleaned out?"

Yes, by a very tall Asian medical student. The wax drill felt like a frozen jackhammer. I blubbered like hell and they gave me a Tootsie-Roll.

"Nope," I said. "Can't say I have."

"Well," Burk said, and he scratched his neck. "My aunt used to do the home kit. Little blue squirter thing. Like hydrogen peroxide? For swimmers. It was for swimmer's ear. But I'm not a big swimmer." He smiled for some reason.

"Sure," I mumbled.

"So my aunt did this too," he said, patting the nub. "I live with her," he added. "Duh, right?" Silence. He tapped his knee. "Yep."

I sat on his bed, the site of untold ear canal excavations and one supposed amateur implantation. New smells. I had to pace my breathing. I didn't want to think about him asleep, taking off more of his clothes.

I looked right at Burk and shook my head. "Dude," I said. "Nobody believes you."

Saying it like that, after he'd begged me into his home, it sounded totally cruel. But there I was, stuck in Jabba's lair. It made sense, somehow. Like his apartment insulted him, so I was free to continue the trend. Who wants to think of somebody that sad loaded with something awesome like an internet nub? I'm not a mean guy. It's not like I toss puppies over fences or anything. But I couldn't stand it.

"No," Burk said. "I never tell people about the earwax thing. Ha ha." He grinned again like, *Stop, stop, dude, come on, just stop.*

But it was out there, so I kept going. "Nobody believes that you can actually see the internet in your head. With that nub. Even though it lights up or whatever."

He sighed. "It's weird."

"How'd you get it anyway? How did you get it from Japan?"

"Off the internet. The real internet."

"Where in Japan? Some gerbil scientist? One of those stem cell dudes?"

He didn't say anything, but faced his computer and began to click around, which annoyed me. "Because nobody fucking believes you," I said.

"Well, everybody looks."

"But that's because it's so weird," I said. "It *glows.*"

Silence. "Okay," I said. "Let's say it works. What does it really look like? In your head, the internet? I mean, you say fuzzy, but shit." I leaned forward. "What does it really look like? You know, what do boobs look like?"

He swiveled in his desk chair, staring down. "It looks sort of like a dream. You know how you stick things in your head, like you tell yourself to think of boobs and they're kind of shadowy? It's like that, but crisper. You tell yourself, get Google. Then all the buttons and icons sort of burn into your mind. Like sunspots, you know?"

"You Google boobs and they're sunspots? Is that what you're telling me? Can you play any games or go on YouTube or anything?"

He shook his head. "It sort of blurs out if I go somewhere too heavy. Too intense."

I laughed. "No MySpace then."

He laughed too. "MySpace works great, actually. I have these friends. From England and Japan and Belgium and stuff. I have this one friend from Belgium who sends me comments about waffles. It's kind of this joke we have. I love waffles. I could eat like a bucket of waffles and then just fall asleep. I could eat that stuff for days."

I didn't know Burk had a MySpace. "Waffles are good," I said. "You sit there in class and go on MySpace in your head?"

"Kind of. Google has this game. Where you tag their pictures with this anonymous partner? It helps the search engine label stuff. Sometimes I'll just sit there and play the picture tagging game. Lots of cars and graphs and stuff, but sometimes, um." His voice lowered. "Sometimes it's totally awesome."

Burk yanked himself up and walked to his closet. He opened the door and pointed to a tiny world map, scotch-taped to the top of a full-length mirror. A little paper map, maybe ripped from a geography book.

"New Zealand," Burk said. "Where they filmed Lord of the Rings. Who doesn't want to go to New Zealand, right?"

New Zealand sat on the map, though I couldn't see it. There was the map on the mirror, Burk in the mirror, nub in the mirror, Burk in the flesh, Burk with his gut, nub in the flesh, nub all red yet somehow shimmering—then me in the mirror, me sweating from the heat and the smell and now from something else, me turning red like the nub, looking at Burk's mirror.

"That's good," I said. "Maybe when you're old. Maybe you can buy a plane or something. So you have enough seats."

See, I was thinking of how they make you buy two seats if you're too— yeah. Why can't you forget these things? Why did I have to look at him? I'd almost forgotten, drifting away, imagining his fantasies all hyped on digital goodness. Why are the real things always quiet and always there?

I stammered, "Because you're gonna score off the nub thing. You're gonna kick ass."

He stared at me, eyebrows going up and down. "It's just to play around. I don't even like computers. It's not—they're okay."

"I know, I know, I'm sorry."

"You know, you have to do a lot of things you don't like. I don't even like the fucking tuba." Burk doesn't usually cuss. He glared out the window. "I don't care if people believe me."

"Yeah, that's cool. You shouldn't." But I couldn't sound sincere. Because if it was me, I know I'd care. If I had to be Burk and sleep my fat ass under his flannel sheets, I would care until the care grew in me like a hot shout, like a bloody mess.

Out the window, I saw a green van pull in. "There's my aunt," Burk said. "There's a few sodas in the fridge, if you want." He sat at his computer. Sweat dribbled from his back fat.

"Hey," I said. "Peter Jackson might make the Hobbit movie too. You think he'll make it in New Zealand?"

"How should I know?" he said.

"You want to look it up? I mean, you want to use—"

His nub hand cradled the mouse. "It's charging."

ↄ

On Friday, the nub looked awful. The glow was gone and a gray-yellow ball of pus sat below the skin. Beet red all around, and my own hand throbbed to look.

We had a special morning recital in the gym, so Snowman Slocum gave Burk some gauze. It was a concert for parents and relatives, a warm-up before the town's annual May parade and a chance to pry some donations from our loved ones. After they've shelled for uniforms and reeds and four years of trips to Canada, they'll usually give us twenty bucks out of muscle memory. Slocum says that many people find patronizing the arts "vitally essential." He likes to repeat this phrase, usually to school boards.

I thought about this as I fiddled with my clarinet's mouthpiece and watched Burk wheeze back and forth between the stage and the bathroom, dabbing his hand with paper towels. If the nub had come from Japan, where did he get the money? He didn't have a job that I knew of. Some national charity helps him with his band stuff. He puts their stickers on his sheet music folders. Indie installation techniques or not, there was no way he could afford even a black-market Japanese nub. I know the Japanese do some weird shit, and I know they like to test it on American teenagers, but there was no way. Before we started I gave Burk a little thumbs up, but he lofted his tuba in front of his face.

The thing went okay. Burk's tuba fell behind the beat a couple times. Ty had a few nasty squeaks. Me? I played my clarinet like a warship on fire. People flung their babies at me. Thank you very much for asking.

At the orange juice and sugar cookie reception, I met Ty's family. His dad was at work, I guess, but he introduced his mother and his uncle. His mother was a hefty lady, crashing around in this purple muumuu and laughing like she was screaming. "I said it already, but you sounded great! Did they record this? I want to go out and buy the recording right now. Where is it? Did somebody record this?" She hugged Ty, lifting him a little, and ran off. The uncle, of beer-giving infamy, wore sunglasses and sniffed his fingers. He would lean down and whisper things into Ty's ear, and they would snicker. I stood there, grinning like the loser I am, wishing to be someone who felt comfortable enough to punch my buddy in the arm.

"Nice notes, squeaky," I said.

"I am Cat Anderson's fucking spirit child," Ty said. "I play that thing like a goddamn piped piper."

His uncle snorted. "Kid, you play like shit." He turned to me. "And you should hear him when he practices," he said. "Lousiest shit I ever heard."

Then he did this weird thing where he sniffed at Ty, like smelled him, and then he laughed and clapped Ty on the neck. Ty stared at the floor. "You can't even hear the trumpet," he mumbled. "I have to go the bathroom."

After Ty left, it was just me and his uncle. "Let's say there are six kinds of fucking people in this world," he said.

"What?"

"They aren't, but let's say there are." He drew from his flask, in the middle of parents and students and League Champion basketball pennants. "Let's say there are six types of people on this Earth. I don't know where I'm going with this. Let's say your sister is a loony for the ages, let's say that her kid sits around listening to nigger music and playing a nigger on his little car stealing game or playing his little queer sword games with his faggot little friends. Let's say that he fights with his goddamn grandma, even when she lets him drive her car." He drank from the flask and stared at the rafters. "Who the fuck fights with his grandma? Man, I love that kid! Don't you know it."

Snowman Slocum walked up, fluttering his hands. "That is completely and utterly inappropriate," he whispered. "Please put that away."

Ty's uncle dropped the flask on the floor, placed one finger on his left nostril, and blew his nose. "There are five other kinds of people," he said. "But there ain't a one of 'em knows what to do about it."

"Do you know this man?" Slocum asked me.

I shook my head.

Ty's uncle turned to Slocum. "Listen," he said. "I'm gonna buy this whole band six pizzas. Save one for the tubby dude with the broken finger or whatever. And this one needs to eat." He swept his hand toward me, sniffled, and nodded several times. "That's what I was trying to say. Six pizzas."

He took a bunch of twenties out of his front pocket and handed them to Slocum, who believes that patrons of the arts are vitally essential. Slocum and Ty's uncle went outside the gym. Then they came back and asked us our favorite toppings.

☙

We all changed and took the free pizzas over to the math teacher's room. As per the code of nerd silence, we mentioned neither Ty's tweaked-out uncle nor Burk's unwrapped and ghastly nub. But we looked so hard and often at the nub that we didn't eat much of the pizza. Ty, who didn't touch one pepperoni, finally groaned. He got up, grabbed an entire pizza box, and chucked it in the trash. He walked over to Burk and stood above him. "Alright," he said. "What the holy fucking fuck?"

"What?" Burk said. He was on his fifth slice of sausage and mushroom.

Ty started counting on his fingers. "It's not a fucking magic nub. It's not some weird Neuromancer brain implant. I mean, look at it." He shuddered, did it extra hard because we were all watching. "You can't honestly tell us that thing isn't a tumor or cancer or something. It doesn't even light up anymore! You can't honestly tell me you're still seeing the fucking internet in your head."

"Actually," Burk mumbled. "I see it better than ever." He closed his eyes, but his voice rose. "You know what I'm doing right now? I'm multitasking. I have Everquest in one window and I'm watching YouTube. I'm watching this Swedish dance group."

We went wide-eyed. "Bullshit," Ty whispered.

"You can believe me if you want," Burk said.

"It hurts, right?" I said. "It hurts."

"If you want," Burk said.

"I call bullshit," Ty said. "That is so much bullshit."

"What does the dance look like?" I said.

"You want me to dance?" Burk said. "No thanks. I can see it just fine."

And he smiled, that wisp of a smile from physics class. A wee little grin, thin as lipstick on a hippo. We all stared.

Except Ty. He jolted away and ran over to the math teacher's desk. The teacher was out somewhere, but he trusted us because we all liked math and being quiet. Ty rifled through the desk and yanked out a protractor.

We watched—tired from the recital, creeped out—as Ty darted to where Burk sat. Then, in one of those moments when noise drops away to your own thudding and wheezing, he stabbed Burk's hand. One clean thrust.

Burk's eyes flashed open. But then they closed and his face went white. You could almost see the scream grow, see it rise from the middle of his stomach and end all around us. He toppled, his tiny plastic chair flying from under him, like he'd lost to a bulls-eye in one of those fairground dunk tanks. Squished, tangled among chair legs, he just lay there and panted.

For a minute, nothing moved. Sound came only from the outside, a low static of catcalls, laughter, cussing. Ty heaved these big jagged breaths that were almost funny. Then he reached down and touched something. When he rose, he held out his finger. Red goo. "From his hand," he whispered. "From his fucking nub. It's just blood."

We shuffled our eyes. Ty had pimples and pale arms. But we said nothing. I remembered Burk's messy desk and his earwax bed and thought about how disgusting people can be. How do poor people get fat? How many kinds of people are there, really? Why can't we just see things in our head whenever we want? Especially when there's nothing else for us. But I didn't say anything. Geek-geek hurrah: dignity in clean computer desks, dignity in silence and ignorance and the trudge forever through the blush.

Ↄↄ

Burk was absent from school for a week. When he came back, his hand was wrapped in gray athletic tape. We didn't talk to him. Snowman Slocum made Ty lead trumpet, and we got a new travel bus with TVs above every seat. Burk must have said it was an accident, or maybe everybody else knew the nub was just a weird cyst and figured it had popped of its own accord. Ty did play in the musical, but we stopped hanging out. I deleted all my computer games, even the SNES emulation ROMs, and started reading about ancient civilizations. Turns out the Greeks and the Romans did all sorts of stuff besides sleep with little boys.

But that's not even funny to me now. Pretty much every time I make a joke it makes me sad, which I guess is attractive or something because I'm going to go drinking next weekend with a bunch of emo chicks. We're going to sneak into a movie. Maybe climb the railroad bridge and drink some Hot Damn.

Now, every time I walk home, I see Burk. Maybe he's always been there. I never say anything. Maybe I should buy a bike so I won't even have to look. But last week I happened to glance over, saw him waddling into his parking lot. And I felt like shit, so I nodded.

When I tell this story, I talk about the stabbing, but I don't say what I saw. Just before he fell. Some say they saw nothing and some aren't sure. But me? I saw buttons and icons. Windows and links. Right there in his eyes, bright as sunspots. Show me all the blood you want, but I saw what I saw.

LOOK! LOOK! FEATHERS

LOOK! LOOK! FEATHERS

We found the baby in the medicine cabinet. Kid smelled like hickory and something else. Deodorant? I creaked the cabinet's joints and witnessed a three inch baby yawn and grump and paw the air with an experimental baby fist. Then I shut the cabinet and bit my knuckles. "Jesus fuck," I said, and my wife, Johnnie Mae, said "Do what?" She was standing in the bathtub with a screwdriver, cleaning the showerhead of pebbles and silt. Her jeans were rolled up to her ankles. She wore a sports bra. I pointed at the cabinet. She gouged the showerhead. "What'd you do to the cabinet?"

You'd think Johnnie Mae would've heard him when we walked in. Maybe smelled him. She's good like that. If this doesn't come up later, I met Johnnie Mae under the televised grace of a long throw by Steve Young to Jerry Rice in the 1994 Super Bowl. This was at the Nugget, which has since shut. Used to be you went there already sorry for something, pretending to get less sorry and practicing to get more. After Rice crossed the goal line, I high-fived Johnnie Mae. Next day, I took her out for steaks at the Run Off Grill. She lost an earring in my truck, called after I dropped her off, and I drove back to her place so she could crawl around trying to find it. "So great, I'm blushing," is what she said, and I studied her ass as she quested. "Babe," I said. "This is good luck." Then she sat up on her knees, looked at me, and combed her fingers down my beard until they rested on my neck. She squeezed. "Yeah, good luck."

But luck, really, is for squinters and liars. Nobody else wants near the shit. What our luck gave us was this: the ex-medicine cabinet of Kheng and Cassie (major pain, almost needed the sheriff to evict 'em) where a fuzz-skulled doughboy now gurgled on the bottom shelf, head no bigger than the toothpaste cap beside him. Johnnie Mae said "That a doll?" and took a better look. Then she crossed herself with the screwdriver. She took a bushel of sanitary wipes from our kit. Swaddled the baby in those, like how you might save a ladybug.

"Aren't those chemical?" I said.

"They're the soft kind." She squinted at the baby, flexing her palm around him. "Boy. Can't hardly see his little dawdle, but it's a boy."

I don't know what I was expecting, but Johnnie Mae's face kept all crinkled. She didn't coo or glow. What she did was sit on the toilet lid and give the speck-tike her pinkie to gnaw. She whispered for me to go outside and call Townes. He owned the apartments we managed and didn't pay us any extra to scrub grout. But he also didn't pay anybody. This left us to ape the work of professionals in abandoned apartments. Per typical, Johnnie Mae dropped the elbow grease—mopping, busting cobwebs, bombing the stove, snaking drains—and I watched industrial cleaner foam. And yodeled. And snooped. Kheng and Cassie had left light fixtures full of dead silverfish and a carpet of cat piss. Dented forks and freezer smells. Most impressive: shapes, big polygons, squiggled in permanent marker all over the walls and sometimes involved in geometry. Johnnie Mae had a hell of a time ragging that shit off. She made me help, even. We got a little high off our products, but I turned sober as a toothache watching this tiny baby fuss itself in Johnnie Mae's hand. She kept the other hand underneath. Like a trapeze net, I guess. When I started to call Townes in the bathroom, Johnnie Mae shook her head. *Too loud,* she mouthed. She looked at the baby, back at me. *Right?* she mouthed.

On the stoop outside, I interrupted Townes's afternoon racquetball. "Wish I still had a pager," he huffed. "There's my Christmas list, Waylon."

Of the people who elect to call me Waylon instead of Len, Townes is the only one safe from my love. Very safe. I asked if he remembered Kheng and Cassie, and he grunted. "Out of the question," he said. "In fact, I'm making a milkshake out of their goddamn deposit, all the shit they caused me."

"Not the issue," I said. "Listen. They left a kid in the apartment."

"Hold up," Townes said. I could hear him leave the echoes of the racquetball court. "Like alive? Tell me alive. Does he speak English?"·

"It's a baby. Kind of."

Townes sighed. "A baby we should probably give back."

"You should see it," I said. "It's the sort of thing you need to see."

"Babies? I'm a baby judge?"

I held the phone to my neck and tried to get calm. Around me, the town was faking a spring thaw. It was blue and cold. Mounds of dirty snow dribbled away into puddles of moon-colored soot. People couldn't decide whether to pull their beanies over their ears. Sun teased down from Mt. Shasta and wind cut right back. Manzanitas and junipers swept the hills, speckled by snow. Everything in Dunsmuir is on a slope, and our apartment complex is nicely propped. Doesn't brush I-5 too bad, and from our stoop I can see everything from sidewalks to boxcars.

Look, I'm no homebody. I've sown my oats. Toked up with hookers in Vancouver, skirted arrest with cousins in the Ozarks. Yet only in Dunsmuir do I sleep right. Hippies say Shasta's made of magnetic lava or some shit, but I say it's winter. Winter in the mountains strands you pretty good, and there's something about growing up in a stranded town. Makes the larger world seem mostly the headache of tire chains. From the stoop, the town looked sweet and humble, and I did not want the stress of introducing freakish bullshit. Keeping life steady is a strain. Often all I can do is close one eye, like I'm measuring, and sometimes I have to close both.

"Don't do any calling," I told Townes. "Just come over and have a look. This baby, well, it's pretty little."

"Is it healthy? Tell Johnnie Mae. Make her fix it up."

"Believe me, she's on it."

"Listen," Townes said. "If you need to buy diapers, peas, whatever—we can pencil that in. We can move the numbers around." He was talking quicker now, and I knew from experience he was probably picking his teeth with his tongue. "Where will it sleep? It can't sleep in the apartment. Not safe. You guys got a crib? Is there a crib in the shed?"

Where the baby slept that night was in our sock drawer. Townes didn't come over until the next day, and when he saw the baby he wanted to call the SPCA, but that night Johnnie Mae arranged a pillow of a needle cushion and a blanket of a wool tube sock. She wrapped the baby in a washcloth, made him a little diaper from the fabric she patches jeans with. We tried to feed him bits of noodle, but he cried. I wanted to feed him some bread, but all we had was multigrain, and I worried he'd choke on the little seeds or germ or whatever those are. What he did like was mashed potatoes, tiny scoops. Johnnie Mae bathed him in a saucepan, and when I tried to touch him, he peed on my finger. The pee felt like an eyedropper of hot water.

"It's not even yellow," I said, watching the streak run. "I kind of want to lick it."

Johnnie Mae guffed and shook her head. "Babies pee clear. Come on, Len. You know that."

Going to bed, she told me the sock drawer was fine, but I had my doubts. "We need to leave it open a little," I said. "For air. And can we hear him? If he needs something?"

"Jesus," she said. She was standing at the dresser, tucking him in. I sat on the bed's edge, shirt off, shoes on. Despite Johnnie Mae's earlier worries, the baby seemed okay with our volume. Quiet, even for his size. Most of what he did was nap. "We'll be right there," Johnnie Mae said, pointing at our bed.

"Let's see," I said. "We should hit the doll aisle. Tea sets. Pacifiers. Tiny mittens."

"He's not a toy."

"I know that," I said. "My brain works better out loud. Gimme some credit here."

She left the sock drawer half open and came to bed, clicking off the lamp and nudging me aside so she could burrow under the comforter. "He's just a little off," she said. "He hasn't caught up yet." She faced the wall. I went to rub her shoulders, but she wriggled away. "No, my neck," she said.

"What do we call him?" I asked, hand on her neck.

She didn't answer. She scraped some plaster off the wall. "Bet he's got a name already," she said. "They come like that."

&

When I met her, Johnnie Mae was working for the Siskiyou County Recreation District, overseeing their more gnarly hiring needs. She hooked up folks fresh from drug convictions with starter work: picking trash along bike trails, mowing grass at rest stops. To tell the truth, I think she got off on the yelling. She yelled at everybody. Mopey Laotian gangbangers. Mullet touters. Guys with prison ink across their jaws. But what she really liked was to bully the mothers. The foul-mouthed mothers, CPS regulars and Section 8 collectors. "Needle-Ass Naureens," she'd call them. "Crackhead Christy Annes." She'd make them clean their hair. "And I told Deseree she didn't need no asshole with a tattoo of a skull on fire." That's what she'd say, and I'd shy from her, flushed. What can I say? Her stride's intense. She's frank about her thermal underwear. Johnnie Mae's a woman I first loved with a high five, and my hand stung pretty good.

Me, I doctor photos for a local studio, mostly airbrushing the pimples of high school seniors, but it beats my old gig stuffing down at the Tulelake Pillow Factory. Even with our forces pooled, we're a duo of associate degrees. Townes owns most of the cheap apartments in town, so when me and Johnnie Mae did the live-together leap, we found ourselves in his racket. We tried to pick okay. The perch, the wraparound porch with only a few boards bent. Building painted beige, not neon or pastel like some of Townes's places, like he thinks Dunsmuir is in downtown Miami. There's even a clanky washer/dryer in the shed out back.

Problem was the company. A few nights in, we awoke to shouts and rumbles. Johnnie Mae likes to drink a little milk and Bailey's to get tired, and her glass was rattling on the nightstand. We thought it was an act of God, but then we looked outside and saw an old truck backing a tractor trailer—bam, bam—into the side of the building. Two women—one in just a windbreaker and cowboy boots, the other in a miniskirt and suspenders—were screaming at the truck and throwing dirt clods. Johnnie Mae opened our window and hollered at everybody to knock it off. Both women looked up and flipped both their middle fingers, and the truck dude—he had a bruised eye—leaned from his cab and spit in our direction, a loogie that got only a little air before splatting on his chin.

When Townes swung by to collect that month's rent, Johnnie Mae cussed him so bad he had to go buy an ice cream sandwich. After he came back and got his money, he asked us if we'd be into managing the place: tidying up, resolving disputes, screening tenants, doing what he called the work of "keeping the rigging tight." He'd wet and combed his hair for this second-try visit, and his belt buckle was big enough to be a lifeboat. We were on the porch and Johnnie Mae pried at a nail with her tennis shoe. "We're talking free rent," Johnnie Mae said, squaring him up.

Townes bit his hand and nodded. "Let's work it out," he said. "Throw some numbers."

Johnnie Mae turned to me. "How much you just hand this guy?"

Because I think of myself as the clever sidekick, I said this: "Not sure, honey. Might need to get it back and count again."

Townes got something out of his teeth and gave it the once over. "I hate this place," he said. "I'd like to see it sunk in a fucking rockslide."

"That ain't the language of business," Johnnie Mae said.

"Half-rent," Townes said. "Some benefits."

Johnnie Mae snorted.

"Tell you what," Townes said. "We'll go rent-free and wages if you do me up an hours sheet. Every month. On the first. And," he said—teeth-digging with his tongue—"only one of you. So both of you do something, it's half hours."

Johnnie Mae held out a hand. Townes turned to me and winked. "Thought she might spit in it first."

"There's more'n spit in there," I said, which didn't make sense, but I gave him my gravest eye. Townes shook his head and slapped Johnnie Mae's palm. Then he pulled some of the cash I'd given him from his pocket. "Glad you didn't count it," he said, handing over a crumple of bills. "Hoo boy. Glad, glad. Spend beautiful days with beautiful friends, that's what I say." He tore his ice cream sandwich wrapper into confetti and sprinkled it on the porch.

So Johnnie Mae quit the Rec District, and if our building were a mouth, you could say we cleaned it out with lye soap. Evicted half the building and fixed the washer/dryer. These days, Johnnie Mae grills prospective tenants and bullies the current ones like she's on yard duty. Not that we're mean. Johnnie Mae won't suffer bullshit is all, which I make known. What people are trying to do here, we stress, is live. Rent in cash. No checks, which bounce. No parties, no drugs, no pets. It's the tidiest I've ever seen my days, and in thanks, I make Johnnie Mae a lot of waffles. When the snow whites us out, we nestle. We get naked under a hill of fleece. Mornings, she teethes each of my knuckles and recounts what she saw in sleep. Matter-of-factly, steeling her voice through the bleakest shit. It's one of love's strangest cruelties, the penance of dream share. Because listening is good. Bring it on, we say. We'll save you. But we don't tell our dreams to be saved from them. And I think Johnnie Mae knows what she's doing when she talks to me in the morning. I'm not even sure she likes to talk like that. Yet she talks, and touches me, and watches my face.

"I don't think it counts," Townes said. He was speaking of the baby, for whom we'd rigged a portable shoebox crib. We were looking at the baby in our living room, me and Johnnie Mae and the baby on the couch, Townes pensive and wheeling in my office chair. "It falls under creature," he said. "That's the jurisdiction of the lost pet department. What's that? FIFA? PETA?"

"Trust me," I said. "It's a kid."

"Which is also the name for a goat," Townes said.

"We'll call Kheng," Johnnie Mae said. "Legally, we got to give all their stuff back, anyway."

Townes shook his head. "With legally, it's not like that. It's more swishy."

"It's not like they left a VCR," I said, holding up the shoebox, where the baby was doing his whoa-there act: eyes daunted and roaming, curly-testing his fingers and tongue and nostrils, all so delicate and skeptical. Everything fresh to his register, from our ceiling fan to his own body, which the shoebox so happened to dwarf. "He's not a goat," I said, putting a hand on Johnnie Mae's knee. "And he isn't stuff." Johnnie Mae looked at me and crossed her legs over my hand.

"Well, it doesn't matter what we think," Townes said. He wheeled to the door. "You guys need to keep it until at least Friday."

"Not it," I said. "Him."

"Friday?" Johnnie Mae said.

"That's when the dinner is," Townes said. "I told my mother about the baby, and she wants to have you over on Friday. For pork chops." He muttered this not easily, which made sense, owing to the magnitude of the invitation.

"Damn," I said.

Johnnie Mae took a little to take things in, and then she said, "We need to bring anything?"

Townes pointed at the baby. "Just our little customer." He creaked upright from the office chair and tried to touch his toes. He grimaced. "Advil," he wheezed. "Advil. Excedrin."

I put the shoebox in my lap and stared at the baby. He made a half-pipe with his tongue and didn't look sure of anything. Johnnie Mae got up, opened the front door, and waited while Townes coughed.

❧

Railroad tracks, cut into the canyon above, rim the town. Below them, the second highest building's the old depot, now a classy microbrewery. Highest is Townes's house, a three-story Victorian built as a convent, abandoned when the nuns got modern. Townes bought it from the Catholic school and towed it to our uppermost ridge. His moving operation tangled several power lines, which left folks to sit outside with parade supplies—hot chocolate, corn dogs—and spectate. Now Townes lives there with an infamous backyard and a dying mother. They've got the best vantage around, though I never see her outside, and mostly I see Townes in the yard.

That yard—it's something else. Goes beyond a junk fetish. Townes has artificial cactus and baby ostriches. He ships them off when they turn cranky. He's got wagon wheels, troughs, croquet, bougainvillea. Couple years ago he faked an Indian artifact discovery. Threw some dirt on an arrowhead and called UCLA's archeology department. They dug around for a week before they wised up, affirming our conviction that all of California too close to the Pacific needs a good brain draining. Townes seared bison steaks for the archeologists, but he made them pitch tents. His mother, Dena, doesn't cotton to houseguests. She tricks death by eschewing sun. If Dena weren't still around to wake up and need whatever, Townes would've left Dunsmuir years ago. Instead, he builds shitty apartments and lets them leak. Rents to whack jobs. He plays in his yard or plays racquetball, plays on his speedboat or plays tinkly-ass flamenco guitar at the hippies' open mics. In short, he pisses everybody off.

The week before the dinner, I stayed up late doing leftover Photoshop from the studio. As I worked, the baby kept distracting me. In the wee hours, he didn't come across so quiet. So I burped him and lullabied. Nothing helped. Finally I fed him some fruit sherbet. It stained his mouth pink. He fell asleep. Standing there in the dark, head blunted by sleep lack, I stared at this mutant little thing and felt the air in the room. Johnnie Mae was in bed, sleeping like the point of sleep was to guard your pillow. I wanted next to her. Though it felt shitty, I could understand the impetus of abandonment. Here's a thing that can't much help itself without you, but how far do you go? You can't shrink the world. Those mama birds with the mouth worms—they don't play that game for runts. But I couldn't stop standing, wincing at random noises, wanting to quit my thoughts of this stunted thing and wanting to build myself around them, to leave this thing in a church plate but hide that plate from harm. Staring down at the drawer, holding my measuring spoon and sherbet carton, I felt like harm meant everything. So where's he go then? Where do you leave a thing you can't leave?

When I woke at noon, Johnnie Mae was red-eyed in the kitchen, wearing one of my T-shirts and a baseball cap, stirring a boiling pot. She didn't have any shoes or pants on, and I went to hug her, but she whacked me in the arm with her spoon. Water splashed and burned me. "Shit," I said, rubbing my arm. The burn was plenty red, and I knew it would scab. "I just woke up."

"Rise and shine. I've been up since the middle of the goddamn night with that—with that thing bawling and puking all over itself." She stirred the water. "Throwing up *sherbet.*"

"Where is he?"

"He's fine!" she shouted. "Christ. Take a look. Then maybe you wouldn't need to fucking ask." She turned the burner off and banged a lid on the pot.

I left the kitchen and went into our bedroom. The lights were off, and I smelled fabric softener. Closed all the way was the sock drawer. I took a second before I opened it, because I thought maybe I'd find a zombie baby, grizzly as a walnut. But when I yanked the drawer, there he was: fine, fussing, crying in that silence of his, where you could only see his fit by his face, wet and scrunched.

Since I couldn't find the shoebox crib, I carried him into the kitchen on our pillow. I set the pillow on the table and sat. Johnnie Mae was still at the stove, tapping the lid with her spoon.

"You can't close the drawer," I said. "That's how he breathes."

Johnnie Mae picked up the lid and side-armed it against the wall behind the stove. It made an awful clank—water jumped, hissed the burner—then fell on the stove, jittering on its top. Johnnie Mae whipped the towel off the fridge and began to scrape her hands ferociously. "I know how he goddamn breathes," she said.

"Yeah? You closed the drawer."

She turned, choking the towel at her side. "Well, did I hear him crying in the first place? Well? Did he throw up?"

"Look, you could've got me. I thought the sherbet would be a treat."

"And why is he in our drawer? Why is he in our house?"

"That's our job," I said. I looked at the pillow. The baby's face was even wetter. "Did I ever say I wanted him here? 'Hurrah' is not what I said. I'm just saying that so long as he's here, we better take care of him."

Johnnie Mae pressed the towel into her forehead. "This is our house," she said. "Just because it's in this *place*, this goddamn *place*, that doesn't mean everything is ours to run around taking *care* of."

I rocked in my chair. The sink was full of dishes from the dinner I'd made last night, beef stroganoff, which Johnnie Mae wouldn't let me feed the baby even after the internet said it was fine. Johnnie Mae hadn't brewed any coffee, and her hair was stringy. I realized she probably hadn't taken a bite since she woke, not even a sip of water.

"What's in the pot, anyway?" I asked.

"I don't know," Johnnie Mae said. "I was just boiling." She sat at the table with me. "I cleaned him. Gave him milk. I cleaned his face, but he kept crying." She tugged at the pillow. "Figured I'd try to make something, but I didn't know what to make."

"I can make something," I said.

"Waylon." She shook her head.

I stood and opened the refrigerator, taking out a carton of eggs, a Ziploc bag of bacon, some maple syrup. I lined these on the counter, grabbed a frying pan from the dish rack. Then I lit another burner, holding my hand over the pan to wait for the heat. "I feel good," I said. "About what we have."

"We can't keep him," Johnnie Mae said. "He's not our job."

When the pan got hot enough, I dropped in the bacon. "But we're good at it," I said, watching the sizzle. "Why can't we just keep being good?"

Johnnie Mae didn't answer, and I kept watching the bacon, so I can't say what her face did or anything. But I heard her breathing, and maybe her breathing changed a little. The baby, well, I could hear a few fluffs, him punching the pillow. But mostly I heard the bacon in the pan, and I felt starved enough to eat it raw.

"You'll have to call Kheng," Johnnie Mae said. "He liked you."

Even though the bacon wasn't done, I cracked an egg on top. Grease turned the yolk an ugly color, and blisters of bacon fat popped up through the egg. I poured syrup, which made everything smell maple. "Who do you think's gonna make the pork chops?" I asked, turning around.

Johnnie Mae was biting her nails like a schoolgirl. She bit and sucked her nail and bit again. It was gross. But she didn't stop. She watched me watching her and kept going, sucking and biting. Biting and sucking. Spring was in the kitchen, bright and cool, and Johnnie Mae didn't look like the woman I knew. "I don't know," she said. "Not us."

I walked and sat across from her, taking her hand out of her mouth and putting it in mine. I had to lean over the pillow. "Did you sleep at all?" I said, and the words rippled my lips over her fingers.

"A little," she whispered.

&

Dena had enough candles to buy stock in the fire department. Tea candles, spread where you might expect to find anything else. Bookshelves of tea candles, tea candles stuffed in a spice rack. Dena carried an electric matchstick in her dress pocket. She didn't say anything. Townes had corduroys that ended above his socks. If they'd changed furniture since the nuns, I couldn't tell. In the dining room, we sat in clawfoots with sheepskin covers that belonged on car seats. For the baby, they'd set an antique high-chair, darkly wooden and wicker-backed. We'd brought him in a cookie tin, plush with washcloths, so we set that in the high chair. When Dena saw the baby she finally spoke: "God alive," she said, peering. "Disgusting."

Pork chops turned out to mean four frozen dinners—whipped potatoes, soggy green beans, bricks of meat—and a table set with butter, ketchup, tea candles, and a jar of applesauce. "We don't eat pork without applesauce," Townes said. "It cleans the meat."

Dena nodded and tucked her napkin in her collar. She pointed at the high chair. "Did you bring food for it?"

Me and Johnnie Mae looked at each other. "If you have some milk—" Johnnie Mae said.

"Townes," Dena said, "Go get a teaspoon. We'll give him a little applesauce. You don't want to feed it dairy," she said to Johnnie Mae. "That's not people milk."

Townes got the teaspoon, gave it to Dena. Nobody was eating yet, so I snuck a green bean off my plate: cold. Dena gestured her teaspoon at the jar of applesauce, and Johnnie Mae handed the jar to Townes, who opened it and held it for Dena. She scooped and passed the teaspoon to Townes, who passed it to me, and I passed it to Johnnie Mae, who scrutinized the teaspoon like it was a Canadian penny. Townes screwed the lid back on the applesauce. Then Johnnie Mae stood, walked around the table, bent over the high chair, and offered the spoon: the baby gripped with both paws, smacking and gumming, trying to gag himself on applesauce. Johnnie Mae had to tug a little to get the spoon back. She faced us. "I think he wants more," she said.

Dena shook her head. "Colic. Can't feed 'em too much when they're colicky. All they go'n do is barf it right back."

Johnnie Mae sat. "That what colic means, is it?"

All of the wrinkles around Dena's mouth pursed. "Yes m'am," she said.

Only tea candles lit the room. Every window was curtained. Our silverware clinked and our jaws slurped. Townes shoveled his potato mash like porridge, and when he finished his vegetables he licked the juice off the plate. Dena ate one bite every minute and otherwise stared. Me and Johnnie Mae, we ate like we always eat, except we didn't talk or smile. The baby lay perched in his cookie tin, kicking and scooting and scraping the tin against the high chair.

Townes was the first to finish. He held his fork looking for more. Then he turned to me and Johnnie Mae. "You guys ever been to Mardi Gras? You know what a king cake is? It's this day old bread and cinnamon. Fried, filled with cream cheese. And inside you stuff a tiny baby. Tiny little plastic baby. And whoever finds the baby—" he pointed his fork at us— "is in charge of the next cake."

"We want it," Dena said. Her hands were in her lap. "With your folks' permission, we'd like the child."

Somewhere below us, a furnace clopped. Johnnie Mae speared a green bean and left her fork there. I realized for the first time they'd given us nothing to drink. Instead of glasses, we had tea candles. The table was made of myrtlewood. Dusty. And the food was shit. Tasted of freezer burn. What I had then, straight from whatever heaven cranks such things, was a vision: the baby as a boy, an elf, dressed in the fatigues of a GI Joe, camping before a tea candle on the surface of the table, nibbling a fish stick crumb, dust mites flocked in his hair, his nights so cavernous and lonesome I couldn't damn fathom. And what if he stayed with us? Me and Johnnie Mae? A sock drawer. A saucepan. She would scold and I would kowtow. Winter would bury and people would hoot. He might say the truest thing he could, but people would barely hear.

"He's not ours," Johnnie Mae said.

"That doesn't mean—" I looked at Johnnie Mae. Her face was set like always.

Townes nodded. "I spoke to Kheng," he said. "He didn't even know about it. Said it was probably some fool thing of Cassie's. She's off the charts, he said. In with monks."

"Monks," I said. If I'd said the word twice, I might've wept.

"Monks can't teach a person to read," Dena said. "Not the monks around here, up in that mountain. They can't teach a boy to scoop tadpoles. Pick mushrooms. Whatever those awful monks do up there, it's not fit."

"If they're the people he's from—" Johnnie Mae said. "Well, I think they've got some rights."

Dena put a finger in a tea candle. "Young lady," she said. The candle went out. She pulled her finger away and wiped it on the table. "They're the people who left him. He doesn't need nothing from them."

"Is there water?" I asked, pushing my plate away. "This a dry house? Is this house a fucking dry house?"

Townes rose and left. The baby was scooting his tin toward the edge of the high chair. I got up and took the tin. Even though I wanted to slam it on the table, I couldn't. The baby's eyes were too big and too small. I set the tin gently. Nobody spoke. I went and got my coat, came back and put my hand on Johnnie Mae's shoulder. "Monks," I said. My voice cracked.

Johnnie Mae set her hand over mine.

Townes returned with a bottle that looked like something out of trench warfare. "It's warm," he said. "Hope that's okay, Waylon."

Dena stared at me. She motioned for the bottle and Townes held it out to her. She clasped Townes's wrist. "When Townes was young," she said. "This place was cleaner. No monks. None of these dopers. Couldn't barely clear the grade if you wasn't a logging rig. Townes's daddy used to take him tobogganing. Hunting. There was a time they went hunting and his daddy shot a bald eagle. Right out of the sky. And far away, such as that they didn't think they'd find it."

"The woods," Townes said.

"Well, they found it all right. And the way his daddy told it, Townes was in a state of rapture. Plucking feathers off the bird. Look! Look! Feathers. That's what he said. And he kept 'em all. In a bag."

"They're in the attic," Townes said.

"You ate an eagle," I said.

"We know joy," Dena said. "I'm sorry for what you think of us, but we know joy. That boy—he's no different. Not a different thing about him. We've got plenty of joy."

Johnnie Mae stood and took hold of my arm. "Good food," she said. "Much obliged."

I let her lead me from that house. We walked downhill. Outside the gas station, kids in ski pants were goofing off, dropping candy bars down each others' crotches. Marquee aglow, the town theatre was helplessly hokey, spooling films we could watch for free on the internet. Hoboes congregated near the rail yard. Dunsmuir's one of the few towns where all the old train semaphores still stand, though nobody uses them. We've got a motel in a caboose. We've got a mountain made of magnetic lava. There's nothing I won't believe if you base it on love. And nothing I will if you don't. That's the man, at least, I'm working to find.

A few months later, we rented Kheng and Cassie's apartment to a warden in the Fish and Game Department. He brought us rent in an oiled leather suitcase. The first month he came to pay, while Johnnie Mae counted the bills and I brought everybody coffee, I noticed the logo on his cap. Valley quail and a golden trout. Beautiful is what they were. Stitches so tight. Sewing something like that, your hands want to shake. But they can't. You can't let them.

LOOK! LOOK! FEATHERS

Susan White and the Summer of the Game Show

We know what we're good for. Trucks of peach cocktail crash, spill syrup from cans. You don't slip, you clean up. Boys know to nick the tire from a rope swing and hustle to the Forebay, glug to Jay-Z and Alan Jackson and maybe get some ass. Old folk double down and get fond. It's something like the bottom of a tank top brought up for sweat. One kid might search for Big Lem's BBQ Shack Rap on YouTube, 0 hits, and sling it on there himself. We're anti-weather and pro-smoking. Not so prone to fools. Which is why we don't much talk about the summer of the game show, when Delbert Cray and his yahoos moved into the condemned hotel, built a set in the ballroom, and just about boiled the sense in our heads.

He showed up in March outside of Safeway. Like where you might sell baked goods, but all he had was a stool and a TV tray full of questionnaires. If you filled one out, you got a complimentary flashlight, which he pulled from a black duffel bag under the TV tray. Cray was a skinny dude with an apple face, blonde hair in a Jew-boy 'fro he kept pretty neat. Every day he wore high-tops and neon suspenders, not just bright but glowing off a real gas.

He didn't bark you over. Just sat there until you wandered by and picked up a questionnaire. Then he asked if you were good at anything. Well, sure. Plenty. "Think me up a list of five things," he said. "Like toss out the iffy shit and give me five keepers." And people put down the questionnaires and thought. Bryan Colby said paintball, Kristina Saiz said cooking salmon. Mr. Diaz recited a poem in Spanish. Blue Dave had to rub his hat on his face and say he'd be right back, but when he came out of the store he walked right up to Cray and said shaving. "Smooth as fucking flint," he said. Cray said that was fine. "It's easy now," he said. "I'm with a new media company called Local On. We're starting a series of television shows in small communities all over the country. Local-On.com. What we do is provide straight up, high gloss entertainment that involves people in the community."

To his credit, Blue Dave gave a real squint. "You out of San Francisco or something?"

"No hippie shit," Cray said. "No politics. Stuff people like: talk shows, game shows, singing."

"Who's paying for it?"

"Well, the overhead's pretty low. All the shows are broadcast on the internet. I mean that's the It now. High res, watch in your bathtub."

"And what," Blue Dave said, "we pay to go on?"

"No, sir. We pay you. Or, I mean, you win what you win. And what happens is local businesses pay for a few commercials. Get their product at your face. And we hire up local kids to be key grips and whatnot, show 'em round the in and out, and pretty soon it transmigrates"—he made a mill wheel motion with his hands—"into being all you. We move out and you've got yourself a nifty little local TV station. High as tech gets."

Blue Dave clasped his hands behind his head and smacked his lips. "Goodness of your hearts," he said.

Cray smiled. "This day and age, we've got the tools to get back neighborly. For a while it was all about watching people on the beach, and that was cool. But why not the biology teacher? Can't she sing?" He raised his eyebrows. "Can't she fucking sing? And that sandwich shop downtown, can't it make a sandwich? Why should we watch some schmuck between shows on ABC try to sell us seven-calorie birdfeed, when you could be going downtown and eating some local-ass roast beef? What's your name, sir?"

"David," Blue Dave said.

"David, let me be straight. This town of yours is paying us. Real money. They're setting us up in that old hotel on Mason Street. What we're selling them is revenue recirculation, people walking to shops they live by instead of driving to God knows where. People talking to the people next to them."

"And paying taxes."

Cray laughed. "Well, I'd imagine that's how they're paying us. I mean, to be straight with you, it's like you've already signed up."

Blue Dave huffed and took a questionnaire. He saw that it didn't ask for his social security number, or even his phone number, which surprised him. He read a few questions. "How long can I hold my breath underwater? Can I drive a stick? Am I allergic to nickel?"

"It's all there," Cray said. He reached into his duffel bag and handed Blue Dave a flashlight. "You can fill it out online if you want."

When we compare notes, what we do admit is that Cray never lied. The city had indeed found him, not the other way around. There was some kind of thumbtack in our socks that year. Maybe because the Parade of Lights got rained out. All the rain, in fact, which cast a smell of rotten cranberries over most of winter. Truth was, people were putting more allspice in the persimmon cookies, paying their gas bills a little later, and—at the same meeting they finally approved the skatepark—voting 5 to 4 for Delbert Cray's Local-On.com Local Entertainment Empowerment Service.

Local On started with green tarp and scaffolding. It's actually pretty fun to walk under scaffolding. You hold your coffee tighter and feel important. Maybe wish for nifty sunglasses. But when you talk about scaffolding over ham salad and coleslaw, you frown. Susan White and Kathy Morse, in a booth at the Blueberry Twist after Thursday tennis, set about agreeing with each other.

"It's just there's a way things go," Susan said. "Isn't there?"

Kathy nodded twice. "The whole thing's a little screwy."

"Why do we need some YouTube channel to come in and—it's like renting a circus to organize the prom. We're plenty good at helping ourselves."

"Exactly," Kathy said. "The irony of the thing, of course, being that the community radio station is already right there next to the hotel. And they do a terrific job. That interview show."

"Their antenna's already on the hotel!" Susan said, widening her eyes emphatically.

"Pierce and his friend might get a show," Kathy said. She spread butter onto a roll. "They talked to the lady. They want to play local emotional bands."

"Emo," Susan said.

"What?"

"It's not called emotional."

Kathy shrugged. "I'm still a jam in the park girl. Ladybugs, you know. Bare feet."

"It's like goth but not as medieval," Susan said. "Reynard sent me a mixed CD for my birthday."

"Isn't he a little old for emo?"

"He's not a *fan*. But he explained it."

Susan had DJ-ed last year's Safe Grad Night, an event held at the local gym where high school seniors could party after graduation: swim, climb the rockwall, have pie eating contests, all an alternative to quarry kegs and car crashes. Kathy, president of the school board, did most of the Night's behind-the-scenes work. When it came to the fun, however, she counted on Susan to steer. A lot of us did. Susan White was not just the librarian. She also organized tennis tournaments, invited national dance troupes, ran a model sailboat club, acted in plays, convinced people to actually watch plays, and spearheaded a First Mondays Nature Walk, correctly surmising that an Art Walk wouldn't exactly fly. Susan's son, Reynard, worked for a punk label in Oakland. For her birthday, he'd wrapped her mixed CD in a t-shirt that read HIPSTER MOM OF THE YEAR. With her son gone and the house to herself, we always saw Susan on the bustle, and we liked when she winked at us.

Kathy's husband, Avery, sat down. He shook his hands dry. "Fan of what?" he said, tucking a napkin into his collar.

"Well, certainly not Delbert Cray's television nonsense," Kathy said.

Avery reached over Kathy's lap and took half her biscuit. "I put down tennis," he said. He chomped and grinned. "Aced 'em all today, that's for damn sure. Even you, Susan!"

"You filled one out?" Susan asked.

"Everybody filled one out," Avery said.

"Don't you remember," Kathy said to him, "when the State Theatre started showing movies again—you remember this—and we took Pierce to see *Honey I Shrunk The Kids* because they'd been promoting it for weeks? New renovation. And then they couldn't get the projector working and wouldn't let us inside—left a bunch of kids crying out there in the heat—and we had to drive over to El Rio to see that reindeer movie?"

"Wait, what heat? That was a Christmas movie."

"I didn't fill one out," Susan said quietly. She reached into her tennis bag and pulled out a folded piece of paper. "I've been carrying it around with me."

Avery set down his biscuit. "Let me see that," he said, taking the paper. He unfolded it and frowned. "It's blank?"

Susan shrugged. She cut a piece of ham but didn't eat it.

Under the table, Avery touched Kathy's knee. Kathy clapped. "You're one of the most talented people I know," she said. "You're like the bubbles in the water!" She pointed at her hair. "You are, for one, responsible for the beautiful color of this hair, which has led Avery to tell me things he's never told me."

"Honey wheat," Avery said.

"And just last week, last *Monday*, Pierce was talking about when

Reynard would babysit him and you would play piano for them. How you and Reynard were probably the first people to get him into music."

"It's not about what you can do," Susan said. "It's about what you're good at."

The Blueberry Twist had no TV, but it did have a pinball machine near the front, tucked next to the racks of real estate catalogs and classified booklets. Multi-level carousels of jam sat on each table. Every Saturday, Shopping Cart Charlie came in and asked for three salt shakers. Corned beef hash and three salt shakers. The rest of the week he sat on the steps of the post office and ate what looked like cat food, though we never got a good look, and certainly we never asked.

"It's a lousy idea," Avery said finally. He cut a boiled egg in half. "It's a God-awful, incipit idea."

"You should be the first one on it," Kathy said to Susan. She leaned in. "You should see how much the cannery donated to the prize pot."

"It's for young people," Susan said, snapping the sweatband on her wrist.

"Look, they haven't even said how it works," Avery said.

"I sent Reynard their website," Susan said. "He said if I get on the show then he'll post a link on his blog. A lot of people read his blog. He posts songs and people go there to get the songs."

Kathy spooned some coleslaw onto Susan's plate. "We'll probably have to mail order you a dress. I can't imagine anybody in this town has what we'll need."

But Avery was right. Local On kept mum on details. We guessed, sure. Plenty of rumors whiffed around, from the hardware store to the cereal aisle. New shifts gabbed with the shifts getting off. Dentists theorized uninterrupted. Lifeguards at the YMCA put a thoughtful finger on their sunblock. All five Lackey brothers smoked pot in the bathroom of the cineplex, argued and boasted and glanced at the smoke alarm. When Joey Worton got a package from New Zealand, the clerks at the post office took a blood pact, opened the box, suspiciously fingered the scuba flippers within, and made Worton fill out an extra form. Lucas Dapling tried to convince Lily Xiong to give him a blowjob. "That's not a talent," Lily said. She was across the room, naked except for Lucas's Jeff Gordon hat. She tried to look at her eyes in the mirror and avoid the forehead zits. She'd read somewhere that people generally just look at your eyes. "It might not even be a talent kind of show," Lucas said, lying on the bed. He jerked off into the pillow a little. Lily snorted. "What is it, a blowjob show?"

Even way out in the almond groves, we got distracted, dropped a handful. In the Pioneer Museum, which no one ever visited, we didn't answer the phone. We watched van after van pull up to the hotel, unload cameras and tile, floodlights and ladders. Sweat began to camp in our brains. Had they really just driven an antique Bentley into the lobby? Did that van really say LIMITED EDITION DINOSAUR BONES?

Then one day, like rice field smoke, the words spread: "First of August." And then: "Email. If you signed up, check your email."

Hell in a handbasket, was it ever on! We got the most expensive haircuts of our lives. We tap-danced in the tool shed. Blue Dave filled his sink with aftershave and dunked his face. Avery yanked out all his heirloom tomatoes and polished them with a rag and a bottle of olive oil. Mr. Diaz dabbed hair gel on the corners of his mustache and rolled his R's. Yahoo, Gmail, Hotmail, AOL: hundreds of technical supporters sighed when they heard our zip-code. "It's working," they said. "All the servers are working. Yes. If you had a message, you'd see it." If you dropped our hearts from the bridge that month, they would convulse to shore of their own volition. If you asked us something urgent, you might be asked to come again.

Susan White was wearing oven mitts when the phone rang. She set her pan of baked peppers on the counter. But this made her nervous about burnt linoleum, so she grabbed the pan and dumped the peppers onto a plate, toed open the oven, and tossed the pan back inside. "Coming!" she shouted. The phone continued to ring. Where was it? By the TV? No, in the bathroom.

She sat on the toilet and answered. They asked if she was Mrs. White. No one had called her that since her husband died. It threw her off.

"Are you there?" they asked.

"Susan," she said.

"Susan, this is Delbert Cray from Local On. I know this is short notice, and I know it's not how we said, but these servers, fuck, these servers. Uh, you good to go?"

"What? Go where?"

"Can you, being Susan White, make Susan White appear on our initial episode of Keepers?"

Susan put the phone to her chest. She looked at the toilet paper and unrolled it a little.

"That's the show?" she said finally. "I mean thank you. Yes."

"Boom. Sweet. Hey, thank *you*. Okay, let's talk logistics."

"Should I get something to write with?"

"Negatory. No writing. Keep it in the hush puppy. Secret! Builds hoo-ha. Like, the name of the show, right?"

"Keepers?"

"Except you don't know that. Everything I'm about to tell you, you don't know."

And Susan White, DJ of Safe Grad Night and leading lady in most all of the Birdcage Community Theatre's productions—especially the ones with singing, had no problem being coy, even a smidgen aloof. That's why we didn't suspect anything when she walked out of Safeway with a bottle of peroxide and a bottle of champagne. No extra suspecting, anyhow. How could we suspect Susan White when Carla Fowler was kicking little kids off the swing set in a bikini, trying to swing in arcs of feet high as field goals? When Abe Werter was drinking bee pollen and carrot juice? He took us outside The Boss, wiped the burger grease off his apron, and showed us a half-dead cardinal he'd stashed away in a fry box. He scooped it out, cupped it in one hand. Squeezed. Opened his hand. "Glitter," he said.

Sirs and babes, we had our thoughts in a twitch. Nothing was looked at; it was sized up. Will this help me snag the nod? Is my dream hot enough? Bless her heart, but we had no room in ours for Susan White.

So she prepped alone. Sat in her living room, practicing scales on a Casio. Wrapped her neck in scarves and recited from Streetcar Named Desire. She cancelled lunch dates. Not that we noticed. Kathy shuffled her plan to buy Susan a dress fatally down her to-do list. With our heads pent up, tennis was a grim affair, and Susan's absence didn't even ping. She stamped books without recommending any. Bought her coffee with less and less chat, then started to carry a thermos. Meanwhile, the fervor about our Local On debut spilled beyond town. One night on Gmail Chat, Reynard (the only person she'd told) let her know that the story had hit Gawker.com.

Hi Reynard!! she chatted back. *What's Gawker.com???*

it's like this gossip website. usually it's just for stuff in new york.

Whoa! Looks like we hit the big time. =)

haha yeah. u guys are local-on's first like whole town thing. i think they've only done neighborhood stuff b4.

So if I mess it up they're out of business huh??? >=)

lol you're not gunna mess up mom!! you rock!!

Susan tapped a space on her keyboard without any keys. She smiled. Reynard explained how he was trying to get a ride up from the Bay Area to see her perform, but he wasn't sure.

anywayz i will watch you on their live feed thing if i can't. hey if u win you can pay for me to take a train up there hahahha ;)

Susan watched Reynard's emoticon turn right-side up and burst into yellow, a full cartoon wink. She wanted to ask him how he'd done that, but she didn't. They chatted, then he had to leave for a gig. He signed off. For a few minutes, Susan sat there highlighting the text of the chat. Clicking it off and highlighting again.

That night, she practiced harder than ever. We all heard her. One thing we didn't understand was why she turned on every faucet and ceiling fan in the house. We chalked it up to nerves. Like the rest of us, we figured, Susan White just couldn't wait for the game show.

On the first day of August, the tarp didn't part until sundown. Though no announcement had been made of tickets, we were lined up and ready. Most of us believed the contestants wouldn't be picked until show time. Nobody wanted to babysit, so we saddled our elderly with the babies and tried to explain how they could watch us on the computer screen. No, you don't need to put a CD in. Just click Refresh and wait until you see us. Outside the hotel, the air was rusty. Hot wind and orange light. It smelled of burnt banana pudding. We mulled, gnawed toothpicks, and waited for the doors of the condemned hotel to beckon us into our obedience to applause cues, or—please!—into the chairs or buzzers or contraptional doohinkees of sweet competition itself.

A little after eight, still not quite dark, the tarp rustled and Delbert Cray walked out of the hotel. He carried his duffel bag and was flanked by two husky black women wearing cowboy hats. They were dressed in white cocktail dresses. Cray looked just like the tarp except brighter, electrified. He wore a lime green blazer, unbuttoned, with a green polo underneath, a huge plastic rose tucked in the breast pocket. He craned his neck and saw how far the line went. He clucked and reached into his bag, pulling out a bullhorn.

"Sorry about the tarp," he blared. "We've had some site issues. I don't even know how to fucking spell asbestos. But the important thing! The important thing is that we're here and we're ready for your—*your very own*—debut episode of Keepers!"

We cheered. Keepers! It felt dramatic.

"Now, just single-up the file there. That's right. We've got your names on our list. If you filled out a questionnaire, you've got a helluva seat. One thing we do fucking right by is our seats."

Squawks of protest rose from those who hadn't filled out questionnaires but who'd been hoping just to watch. Cray compromised with the whiners by wheeling out an enormous monitor, so they could sit outside and watch. Some people had their laptops and watched the online feed. Others passed around red cups. People went next door to the radio station and asked if they could use the microwave. Maybe some of them got bored and went swimming, who knows?

All we knew was the gasp we made inside the hotel. Mr. Delbert Cray had not scrimped an inch. That ballroom was slick as shit. New chandeliers and gussied up wood. Spotlights that darted around like little kids. He'd replaced the parquet floor with carpet and banks of cushy recliners, all replete with cup holders. In back were the refreshment tables: platters of cheese puffs and cold cuts, bottles of local brews in deepfreeze vats. The room smelled like paint varnish and shampoo. People with intense eyebrows ran around, adjusting things and taking us by the elbow. We didn't recognize any of them. They asked us to turn off our cell phones. In the corners were bearded men in tuxedos, each playing a different instrument: stand-up bass, fiddle, slide guitar. They played the melodies of pop country hits. We couldn't find the drummer. Above us, a balcony jutted out, rimmed by flashbulbs and labeled in blue neon: !!! J E E P E R S K E E P ER S !!! We couldn't remember whether the balcony was new or not.

We milled around glugging brews. Made cracker sandwiches. Gave our last wheezes of speculation. Then, after one particularly hearty twang, the band fell silent. The chandeliers flickered and dimmed. We hustled to our recliners. Tapped our feet. Delbert Cray emerged from the balcony curtain. When the lights hit him, we applauded.

"Locals!" he cried. "Locals and viewers all over the world! Welcome to the inaugural episode of Jeepers Keepers!"

Canned piano jingles started up. We whistled and kept clapping. Cray stepped back and the curtain rose to show a pretty homey looking talk show setup, desk and a couch. The backdrop, we saw, was a mural of the whole town: almond groves, schoolyards, supermarkets. We squinted and looked for our houses.

Cray sat down at the desk. "Let me introduce our contestants. First up, you know him by the color of his spirit, the drawl of his whiskey epiphanies, and the photos of his ex-girlfriend he'll show you after last call: Blue Dave!"

We laughed and applauded as Blue Dave sprinted out in a tracksuit, slapping his cheeks and throwing fake jabs. We didn't mind Cray making fun of Dave. We actually liked him better for doing it: made him seem less smarmy and more in the family.

"Next," Cray said. "She's smart as a whip and sweet as whipped cream. You've seen her washing cars to raise money for 4-H, and you've maybe wanted to see a little more: Lily Xiong!"

Lily wore a mini-skirt and a black cardigan. She waved. In the audience, Lucas Dapling high-fived his best friend.

"And, batting cleanup, the kind of gal you want to run the fireworks, the one who finally convinced you to stop drinking bottled water, a woman who seems to plant an apple tree in all of us: Susan White!"

This time our applause made a sneak attack: the tentative, initial *Whoa,* then the heavy cavalry of *Yeah! Hell yeah!* Avery swallowed his gum and grabbed Kathy's arm. Kathy unbuttoned the top button of her shirt and whispered "Well!" Watching with his friends in an Oakland living room, Reynard hoisted a PBR.

Susan, for her part, walked calmly onto the set in white culottes. She blew a kiss to the camera.

All three sat down on the couch next to Cray's desk. In our seats we mimicked them. They crossed their legs and so did we. Cray shuffled papers. He reached under the desk and handed what looked like video game controllers to the three contestants.

"First round," he said. "Question one."

The backdrop pixelated into a picture of an old baseball team. Cray pointed at the picture. "What year did your local baseball team, the Peach Cans, play their last game as a semi-professional baseball team?"

Blue Dave thumbed a button and beeped in. "'57. October of '57."

The slide guitar whanged and the set bulbs flashed. "Bingo!" Cray yelled. "That's a keeper!" We cheered.

The baseball team dissolved into a picture of a Native American in a business suit. "Why did Ishi," Cray said, "the so-called 'Last Wild Indian,' descend in 1917 from the hills into your town?"

Susan thumbed. "He was starving."

"A keeper to Susan!" Cray yelled.

As the first round progressed, we began to feel a little embarrassed. Not all of us, not the fifth grade teachers or the folks from the Chamber of Commerce, but the bulk of us. We had no earthly clue about the most common strain of local wildflower, the details of the dam's construction, which year Bret Harte had visited. Blue Dave got a lot of them, Susan a few, and Lily looked mighty pretty, but when Cray said "Nobody? Nobody?" and the slide guitar played a minor chord, we felt relieved.

Round Two, that's when the trouble hit. First, a sepia picture of an old Union Pacific rail worker blurred onto the backdrop. "How many times does a conductor honk when he drives his train through town?" Cray asked.

"Enough to make me take an Aspirin?" Blue Dave said. We laughed. Lily shrugged, and Susan started to say something but shook her head.

"Okay," Cray said. "New round."

The picture faded into full color, and the rail worker became John Turner, an actual conductor, still driving, living in a trailer near the fish hatchery with his wife, Sylvia.

"How many times does *John* honk to let Sylvia know he's home?" Cray asked.

Startled, we looked around. Neither John nor Sylvia were in the audience.

Lily thumbed a button. "Three and a half," she said. "Like honk! honk! duh-honk!" She looked out at us. We were silent. "My grandparents live down the street from them," she said.

The bulbs flashed. "Lily's on the board!" Cray said. "One keeper to Ms. Xiong."

Next came a picture of Shopping Cart Charlie. Except it wasn't just a picture, it was a streaming video. We shifted around in our recliners. We recognized some of the trucks that pulled up to the post office, some of the overalls that got out.

"What does Shopping Cart Charlie eat every day on the steps of the post office?"

Nobody beeped.

The fiddler yawned. We scratched and scratched our jeans. Inside their vats, the local beers were exactly twenty-nine degrees.

Finally Susan thumbed. "Well, cat food, I guess. Pretty sure it's cat food."

"Keepers!" Cray bellowed. "You're catching up to Blue Boy, Susan! You're catching up!"

In Oakland, Reynard's friends laughed. "Cat food?" they asked. Reynard got another beer. "I never thought it was cat food," he said. "People say it's cat food. I don't know, dude. I mean, they must have the inside scoop or whatever." His friends whooped. "Inside scoop!" they said. "Okay," Reynard said.

All three contestants knew the answers. What could they do but give them? We knew the answers too, especially when we began to see ourselves on the backdrop. Pictures Cray shouldn't have had: locker rooms, late night kitchens. We flitted glances. Blushed and glared. "Did you send him that?" Bryan Colby whispered to his wife. Onscreen he was in the forest, peeing onto a raccoon carcass with his paintball buddies. "You think I've seen that?" his wife whispered back.

"What other animals has Bryan Colby killed so as to piss on them?" Cray asked. Blue Dave mumbled something. "You have to beep!" Cray yelled.

"Dogs, cats and a turtle," Blue Dave said.

"Okay, that's a keeper," Cray said. "But you still have to beep."

There was Mr. Diaz awkwardly strumming, butchering Guantanamera in front of his class. "How many chords does Julian Diaz actually know?" Cray asked, and Lily merely echoed our heads when she answered "Zero." When one of the Lackey's girlfriends appeared onscreen with a different Lackey, a fight broke out in the back of the ballroom. When Marina Rawling's dead mother appeared in her nightgown, taking off her wig and rubbing aloe vera under her eyes, Marina got up and ran for the exit. She pounded on the door, but one of Cray's people hit it with his elbow and it gave. None of the doors were locked. We remembered our old folks watching the show online, and thought to call them, warn them, urge them to turn off their monitors, their computers, flip every switch, but then we remembered all the others watching, all the unknown gawkers, each and every asshole browsing in the bathtub. We jammed our hands into our pockets and sat still.

Up on the backdrop was Big Lem's BBQ Shack Rap. It was pathetic, corn-fed and low-fi. Big Lem looked like the worst kind of fool: funny instead of fun. Cray asked how many views the Shack Rap had garnered on YouTube. Blue Dave guessed thirteen, but he was wrong. Susan buzzed. "None," she said weakly. "Before now."

In the audience, Big Lem's face was red as anything he'd ever cooked.

When Blue Dave himself showed up on the backdrop—passed out on his living room floor, beers and Kraft singles and no lights, Animal Planet on the TV—he jolted up from the couch and leapt onto Cray's desk. He kicked over Cray's microphone. The two black women ran onstage to restrain him. Lily put her head between her knees. Susan folded her hands in her lap.

Cray laughed as the women dragged Blue Dave offstage. One of their cowboy hats fell off. Cray looked directly at the camera. "What a real bunch we've got!" he said.

Some of us began to boo and throw stuff. A bottle broke a bulb. One of the Es fell off the logo. Cray held up his hands. "Hold your horses! We're just in time for the last round."

Lucas Dapling stood on his recliner. "Lily!" he yelled. "This is fucked!"

Lily curled her lip and stared down from the balcony. "You're a *baby*, Lucas. You've got *zits*."

Lucas gawked at her, mouth open, barked a single laugh and sat down. He put his jacket on, popped the collar, and sank deep into the recliner.

Lily walked over to Cray. "Gimme the camera," she said. Cray motioned up at the roof and a suspended camera wobbled down to Lily's face. "Yo YouTube!" she shouted at the camera. "I hope you're having a good day."

And she began to dance. Rap music filled the ballroom. Lily snaked her hips, ran her nails down her body. She didn't look at us. The camera careened and circled, captured her from every angle, and she followed the lens with her eyes like a skeet shooter.

"Register now," Cray said to a different camera. "After Ms. Xiong, Susan White will perform, and then you can vote on your favorite. But you have to click right below this video to register."

Since we couldn't vote, we just watched as Lily stripped off her cardigan, then her mini-skirt, and moved around inside of her own body like molasses. Hands waving above her head, she stood on the couch in nothing but red underwear, swishing her hair back and forth. Some of us realized we'd actually be able to see better if we were watching online, and then we bit our lips and looked down, as if the others might've heard us think that.

One last chorus rumbled through—Lily rubbed the cardigan between her legs—and the rap song faded out. Lily slumped down in the couch and pulled her skirt on, breathing heavy.

Since there was only one computer, Reynard's friends had to take turns registering. Some of them got on their iPhones and did it from there. Reynard sat slumped on his own couch, resting his head on a fist. "Did you *know* that girl?" his friends asked. "She was like, five," Reynard said. "She's fucking hot," his friends said. "I used to lifeguard her," Reynard said. "Those puffy arm things, she used to float around on those." "Damn dude," his friends said, and they made sympathetic noises as they waited to vote.

"Thank you, Ms. Xiong," Cray said. "Now, that was great, and I'm not one to play favorites"—he winked at the camera—"but I woke up from something when I first heard Susan White sing. Susan, would you do us the honor?"

Susan stood and smoothed her culottes. Cray handed her a pair of headphones and she put them on.

"See those boys down there?" Cray said. "Just tell 'em when you're set." Susan nodded. She tapped her feet and counted off.

Fact is, you've likely seen her. We've seen the view counts. Description is just opinion, like how all those people posted follow-up videos after they saw her sing. And we've watched your follow-up videos. We've seen the laptops make your faces glow and heard the air conditioners in the background. And you know what? We agree with everything you said, all the *wows* and *damn girls*. But what you didn't see was how we forgot to swallow. In the video, you can't really hear how we suspended our breath to give her all the room's air. Hell, it was just a country ballad, really. But Susan sang the lights out of it. Her voice was lonelier than sand. She wore those headphones and sang with her eyes closed.

After she took off the headphones, Reynard got up and closed the computer. His friends sat around with their faces down. They picked at the carpet. "Man," they said.

Reynard shook his head. "Country music," he said.

They didn't have to watch the ceremony to know that Susan won. Back in the ballroom, Cray stood on his desk to applaud her. Lily put her head in Susan's chest and Susan stroked her hair, hugged her tight. Then Lily let go and motioned Susan toward the front of the balcony stage. Susan watched us hoot and holler. Kathy stomped and beamed while Avery fired finger pistols. Susan put her hands to her mouth and nodded at us.

We never saw her again.

"Congratulations!" Cray yelled over the applause. "You've won Local On's Dream Migration Grand Prize." He reached under the desk and gave Susan a flashlight and some sunglasses. "Starting today, Local On will use the prize money we've collected from this terrific community to route you anywhere you want in the world. Route you and root you. Susan White!" We cheered even louder. "Susan White!" he screamed. "Where do you want to go?"

She looked at us, then she cupped her hand around Cray's ear and whispered. Cray looked surprised, but he recovered. He squeezed her hand and turned to the camera. "Jeepers Keepers," he said. "Brought to you by—" and the cameras turned for the first time to us. We stared up at them. Though we weren't sure if it was okay to clap for ourselves, we clapped. We couldn't stop.

❧

Not everybody waited outside after the show, so what actually went down is a bit disputed. Truth: Susan never came out. A few of us cornered Cray walking to a van. His jacket was off. His 'fro looked more scraggly than it had onstage, and his makeup was kind of dripping.

"Where's Susan?" we asked. "We want to take her out. Celebrate."

"She's gone," Cray said.

"Come on, Cray. It's our game show. What did you do with her?"

"She won what she won."

"What is this Willy Wonka shit?" we said. "We love Susan, and we're glad she won, but we do have a few things to say about your fucking agenda."

"Agenda?" Cray said. "I like skydiving. I like beautiful women who taste like soap. I like walking up and down the street at night looking for change. What the fuck is an agenda? I'm a service provider. Besides, you're famous now."

"Who cares!" we cried. "You made us look like fools!"

"You guys are reeling in subscribers," Cray said. "What you should be worried about is producing content, not yelling at me." He scratched his 'fro. "You know what I'm gonna do? I'm gonna give you the password to the stat counter. You'll be able to track everybody who watches you. Match IPs with maps. You can zoom in and say that house, that house right there has been watching me sing."

We formed a barricade between him and the van. "It was Susan who sang."

He massaged his shoulder. "Well—it's always Susan, isn't it?"

Far as we know, Cray tried to shove a few of us out of the way, and all we did was shove right back. Of course, that's not what his lawyers said. Plenty of national media outlets covered the lawsuit, owing to our newfangled digital infamy, but we changed the channel on those. Clicked somewhere else.

Cray stacked a tower of cinderblocks outside the hotel, claimed the hotel was his until the city coughed up for hospital bills. He also tried to charge us for the cameras he'd left, said that in the eyes of the law we were still renting them.

We get by like always. When we're too tired to cook, we go to Subway. They show us each step of the sandwich. We ask for the meal, so we can munch chips on the drive home. We wonder about Susan. Even Kathy doesn't know. Her emails bounce. Reynard won't tell us anything, won't visit for Christmas. Doesn't he still have friends here? Sure as hell we're friends, we think, driving. Mostly we cruise straight home, slashing down shortcuts, avoiding the stoplight near the cannery. But we do keep the windows open, keep an ear out for calls. Once in a while, there are people we need to see.

THE WORLD DOESN'T SMELL LIKE YOU

Dudes best reckon. When you conk a mallard, I'm saying make sure it spins, because God spread a helluva backdrop for those birds to cameo around in, and if you're set to fuck with that shit, fuck well. Keep your hair tight. Girls like to feel a neck burr. What I'm saying is buzz the world. Do not let the world buzz you. When folks—usually girls—ask why we didn't show Coach Schiel any mercy, all I say is "Not with me. Your bitching's not with me."

Schiel taught P.E. and wood shop, used the awls in blowjob jokes. "There's plenty of mouths where these don't fit," he'd say, holding the awl and bulging one half of his cheek. "But it never hurts to check." Basketball he coached with the same gung-ho. Always stressing the ease of the shot. How you arc and arc until you've taught your wrist a new way to want itself. And Schiel was obsessed with the goddamn gym floor, keeping scuffs off. We got the notion he'd show up nights in a track jacket and socks, pacing that hardwood to make sure he could see himself in the gleam.

His favorite P.E. activity was homemade. Pygmy soccer, he called it. Every time one team thwacked a goal, some sucker on the other had to tie their shoelaces together. We played this on grass and concrete. When scores rang, democracy bum rushed the selection of lacer: "Shit, that was all Burk! Burk, c'mon. What channel is fucking lard-ass TV on?" Then Schiel would whistle and fake a sigh. "Guess you better tie 'em up, Burk. Why? There's no why in team." And Burk would blush and hobble. Don't get me wrong: we all had our turns to death-lace. It's just some of us got by with looser knots. And certain bastards just shucked their sneakers—God hug the poor fuck who might introduce skepticism of *those* dudes.

What I'm saying is that history class was trying to teach us why we shouldn't celebrate Columbus Day. Mamsy-ass language arts teachers were hinting about mockingbirds and do-I-dare-to-poop-a-peach. But Schiel didn't traffic in such boo-hoo. "Swagger or death," he'd say. "That's how it works. You don't learn how to shake a man's hand, how to grip, I guarantee you'll wake up one night and he'll be pissing in your hair. Why? Why would he do this?" Then he'd wink and pull his wallet from his jeans. Toss it on the floor. "Bunch of Polaroids of my goddamn wife says you cum guzzlers can't tell me why." And he'd wait. Nobody would even close their locker. "That's fucking right," he'd say. And he'd kick the wallet across the locker room, credit cards and gift certificates spilling in a trail. Sonofabitch with his hair slick, smelling of Old Spice, with his love of little mustard packets and his herky pigeon strut. We had something more than mercy. Respect. Somewhere between a mudslide and a mosh pit. That's the sort of respect we had for Schiel.

But the problem was the balls. Word got out about the balls after a horse. Every year, for the Homecoming Spirit Rally, each class had to whip up a skit. Our junior year, the seniors—who'd put in eighteen hefty whacks at life and were feeling all mossy-eyed about shuffling into adulthood's anti-rally of dry cleaning and liver spots—went for broke. Got bolo ties and cap guns, concocted a little soap opera about the rival high school kidnapping Kristina Saiz and hauling her back to their teepee. Or something. Mostly Kristina Saiz's shirt got ripped at the midriff, which definitely accomplished spirit goals. At the peak of the skit, Saiz bound and doomed, Arturo Chavez gamely pursuing his best ooga-booga imitation, the doors of the gym flew wide. And Matt Crane, quarterback and Skoal-chewer of note, rode into the gym on an honest-to-God baby colt. We whooped. Chavez dropped his plastic tomahawk and jogged to the locker room, while Crane and his pony clopped over to Saiz. Crane dismounted, unbound Saiz, and hugged her. She tiptoed and gave him a cheek peck. We arranged our Wrangler bulges. Our thoughts? A survey:

O sweet fuck! Saiz! Tied up by baling wire! Saiz and her sister! Wait, does she have one? Saiz and herself! Twinned! Saiz's snatch buffed in Cool Whip! Like that movie! With my cock all over her lip gloss! Meanwhile, the pony trotted into the middle of the gym floor and took a huge shit.

And then another. Plop plop. Hats off to the equine colon.

Even with the shit, the gym stank of Turtle Wax and teen cologne. Noon light crested the new scoreboard. Pony quivered. Crane and Saiz clutched in a mutual blush, dopey with terror grins, their hug now looking like a bomb drill. Kids began to guff and caw. But most of us boys shook our heads. Schiel was gonna flip. That pony had fertilized the Diggers logo with a steam pile befitting a much larger steed. Eight or nine goops of shit, spread around the Digger's beard and pick-ax.

"Clear out," Schiel yelled. He shoved his way down from his perch in the bleachers, his Reeboks stomping fingers. Down on the floor, Ms. Bishop—home ec, yearbook—was stroking the pony and trying to get it to drink some V-8. Pony flicked its tail and shifted in tiny pivots. "That's a good baby," Ms. Bishop said.

When he got there, Schiel said, "We need plastic bags. Dustpans. Hazmats."

Ms. Bishop frowned. "That boy had no business on top of this poor horse."

"We'll give him a fucking pink slip," Schiel said, puffing his eyes. "Right now, we've got to scoot the damn thing out of my gym."

"He's shivering," Ms. Bishop said. She petted Pony's mane. "He probably won't sleep for weeks."

"Horses!" Schiel yelled. "Horses can sleep! At fifty miles an hour! In a parade! They're goddamn horses!"

Ms. Bishop tried to tip the V-8 into Pony's mouth, but Pony crunched the whole can and spit it onto Schiel's Reeboks.

"Jesus in a fucking jumpsuit," Schiel said. "Get out of my way."

And he tried to shove Pony from the side, which only made it more excited. It whinnied and reared. Schiel slipped and fell, shit smearing his slacks. He got up, went behind Pony, and raised his hand to slap. But you could rule that slap a balk, because Pony gave Schiel the classic barnyard karate: hoof to groin. Schiel crumpled and our chubs deflated as we grimaced in sympathy.

But then things got weird. Quick as his knees hit, Schiel was back up, leaping onto Pony and straddling like a wakeboarder, screaming so hard you could see his spit wiggle. In westerns, horses always give you that big sun-blocker of a leg-lift before they bolt, but Pony didn't bother with any prologue. It fucking booked. Slammed through Ms. Bishop, knocking her on her back. We watched as Pony and Schiel crunched through the gym doors and disappeared outside, Schiel's banshee cusses fading into our collective oh-my-Gods.

We rushed down to Ms. Bishop. She was whimpering, holding her elbow. We helped her up.

"How did he do that?" we asked.

"What?" she said. One arm dangled. With the other, she felt her ear. "Is my ear bleeding?" She fell again.

Abe Sullivan looked down, touched her shoulder, and spoke gently. "We're talking about his balls, Ms. Bishop. We're worried about his balls."

Saiz and Crane came over. Saiz took one look at Ms. Bishop and slugged Crane in the chest. "Pick her up," she commanded. Crane swooped Ms. Bishop off the ground, tucking one arm under her back and the other under her gabardine skirted knees. He stalled. "Um, which way?"

Saiz flailed her arms. "The nurse, the EMT! The fucking 911!"

Ms. Bishop smothered her face into Crane's neck. Blood from her ear dripped onto the collar of his cowboy shirt. He carried her, stumble-skipping, into the boys' locker room.

Saiz looked at the pony shit—still prominent, a little tousled—and pointed at us. "One of you needs to get the janitor."

Okay, my apologies to the narrative scheme or whatever, but: she was mad and sweaty and hella hot.

"Kristy," Abe Sullivan said, popping a grin. "'Sup."

Saiz gaped at us. "Were you born? Are you creatures of sludge?"

Just then, Principal Bernam and Arturo Chavez ran in, Chavez now in street clothes but still with a streak of blue war paint under one eye. "I voted against the horse," he was saying. "I voted a lot."

Principal Bernam preferred to hone his Spirit distant from the rallies. He wore a suit and a Diggers ball cap. Hands on hips, he studied the logo defecation, the stains of V-8 and blood, and Saiz's half-naked hyperventilating. "I'd like a construction," he said finally. "Sort of a classic outline. Bullet points. Roman numerals."

A shriek came from the boys' locker room. Crane walked out very deliberately. His shirt and fingers were smirched with blood. "I'm not into this shit," he said. Then we had to stare at our sneakers, because he started to whimper.

Saiz put an arm around Crane and looked at Principal Bernam. "Ms. Bishop's in there," she said. "In the locker room."

"Of course," Bernam said. "This is good. This is what I mean. Clear statement of fact right there."

℘

Afterwards, in the parking lot, a few of us walked up to Chavez, who was standing outside his F-150, peering into his driver side mirror and trying to tissue off the last of the war paint.

"Is Schiel gonna get fired?" Bryan Colby asked. We squinted under the sun.

"Hell no," Chavez said, blotting. "That dude's a natural force. Besides, Bishop's got a crush on him. She's pissed at us, yo. Not Schiel."

"How did he do the pony thing?" I asked. "How did he not—you know—his balls?"

Chavez laughed. "Ball," he said. "Didn't you know that? Schiel's got one ball. Uno ballaroono. It's like the worst kept secret in the school."

We backed away, stunned. Schiel had only one ball? No way. Was that a joke? We remembered some of Schiel's raunchiest jokes, his crotch grabs, and then we couldn't help but picture our own balls. Dangling, getting snipped, bobbing in a tub like, well, balls.

Ball?

"That," Logan Antin whispered, "is gross."

Chavez turned and frowned. "It's just a ball, guys. He got cancer or some shit. That pony must've hoofed him in the blank spot. Pissed him off." He turned back to the mirror. "You know what position's disrespected? Tight end. Fucking wetback Chavez the tight end. Hey Tootie, you should play the Indian. Really, guys? Don't you think that's a little obvious? Nah man, it'll be a hoot. By the way, how about Matt Sandydick Fucking Crane gets to feel up your girlfriend at the end of the fucking skit? Oh sure. Tootie Chavez the tight end. Skippity doo dah."

We left Chavez to his wiping and jibbering and piled into our vehicles. We drove in silence to Grande Burger. Ordered the tacos. Ladle of steak, squeeze of cheddar, squirt of salsa. Three for a fiver, and they tasted like spicy plastic. We loved them. On the jukebox, boot scooting boogies and gangsta rap traded off, and Mitch the owner had a satellite subscription to every iteration of ESPN. Grande Burger was our cave of fried introspection, our grease fart of a situation room. That afternoon we huddled and reeled and tried not to imagine Schiel's single lump.

"That shit is fucked," Garth Dole said.

"Seriously," we said.

"It's like—" Logan Antin started, and then he punched a napkin holder.

"He's still kind of a badass," Bryan Colby said. "I mean, you saw him on that horse."

"Man, I wanna find that horse and chop its legs off," Abe Sullivan said. "I swear to God I'm gonna eat that horse. I'm gonna put it in my mouth."

"It's not the horse's fault," I said. "Tootie said the horse missed. He said Schiel's been one-balled since—well, he said cancer. I guess that's a long time."

"Don't even say ball," Hunter Limbard said. "I don't even wanna hear the word ball, yo. If you gotta say ball, just say like—" He shook his head. "Ruby. Rubicon or something."

"Dude, that's not a ball," Anthony Whistler said. "That's a castle in France."

"Shut the fuck up," we said. We kind of hated Anthony Whistler. He was too big for his britches.

"We need a plan," I said.

Anthony smirked. "You wanna buy him a new ball?"

Logan grabbed one of Anthony's tacos and smashed it across Anthony's face. Because Anthony was a little bitch, he let the salsa drip down his nose.

"Guys," I said. "On one hand, Anthony drinks his own cum. Okay. Fine. On the other hand, we've got a serious fucking deal. We have to talk to Schiel about this. He has to explain."

"I don't know," Bryan Colby said. "Let him come to us." He burped a cheesy burp. "I don't really want to ask him about his balls."

We grunted. Colby had a point. So we crunched our tacos and gave the situation a stiff lip. Schiel was back at school the next day, and we played pygmy soccer like all was cool. Drilled handles into our cabinets. But Schiel was different. Grimmer, less panache. He'd blow the whistle and say nothing. Wouldn't make fun of the girls in woodshop behind their backs, not how he used to mutter "What is this, lesbian LEGO class?" Now he just said "measure" and walked off.

A few weeks later, Fat Burk caught a soccer ball in the cheek, and Schiel let him hold an ice pack instead of death-lace. Abe Sullivan couldn't take it. He stalked up to Burk in the locker room, yanked away his ice pack, slammed him against a locker, twisted up Burk's P.E. shirt, and dropped the ice down the front of his shorts. Then he held the ice there to make sure Burk could feel it melt. "Piss yourself, fattie," he said. "Piss yourself." Burk's jaw shook, his head tilted back against the locker, Abe's fist bunching his t-shirt at the neck so his gut hung out. A dark splotch bloomed on the front of his shorts.

Schiel came from his coach enclave and pulled Abe off. "Rein it in, Sullivan." His voice was dusty. We wiped our eyes with our P.E. shirts but kept watching. Burk adjusted his collar and plopped onto the bench in front of his locker, legging swiftly into his jeans, shorts left on. A twitch played his shoulders pretty bad.

Abe's face was small and fixed on Burk. "Slob's gotta learn the standards."

"Learning's my thing, Mr. Sullivan," Schiel said. "When I invent your thing, you'll hear."

Abe turned to Schiel. Breath grew and shrank in his chest. Schiel flexed his hand. Benches ran down each aisle of lockers, red and chipped, with initials carved in spots and boogers dried in others. Some of us stood on the benches to see over our lockers. We wore cotton undershirts and farmer tans. Shitty heating vents burped and rattled. The drink machine purred. Usually Schiel liked to keep a tape of classic rock on a loop, but today the office boombox sat quiet. In our open lockers slouched backpacks, messenger bags, name-brand sneakers, and label-stripped soda bottles converted to spittoons for sunflower seeds (allegedly) or dip (copiously). A few boys hoisted their backpacks and skedaddled, ball caps tight to staunch the hair sweat. But most of us waited. Most of our cheeks held a stubble that needed angles to shine, which explained our yearbook photos, the cocked scowls. But Abe's stubble you could see even under the awful locker room florescence, his whiskers unmarred by the drool of light.

"Learning goes both ways," he said.

"Coach," Schiel said.

"What?"

"Learning goes both ways, *coach*."

Abe curled his upper lip. "I don't play on your stupid team."

Boys our age sweat a lot, and the sweat drips. Drops. Sometimes it glistens, like on Burk's neck, which was pale and greasy as mushroom sauce, and Burk sat there with his jeans still unzipped, sweating troughs. Abe practiced a face that didn't sweat. Schiel sighed. He held up one finger. We watched that finger, Abe especially. Schiel spoke loud enough for everybody.

"Boys," he said. "When I was—as they say—young, I wanted girls to look at me and wonder when my birthday was."

He dropped his finger and walked to the drink machine. The school didn't allow sodas, only sports drinks, carbonated equations of power fuel. Schiel opened the machine with a special key, exposing racks of cans. He took a green kind and tossed the can in the air a couple times.

"There's an old love song," he said. "Time goes by so slowly, and time can do so much. Now, there are notes hit in this song by its original singer that make you want to choke the fucker. Just to see if his throat's made of real meat."

He walked back over to Abe and tapped the can a few times against Abe's neck. Then he sat on the bench next to Burk, flipped the can and caught it. Flipped and caught. Burk started to rise, but Schiel pushed him back down. "It's been a rough couple weeks," he said. "Ms. Bishop, as you've no doubt heard, might lose her hearing. Several of our seniors face expulsion, and their graduation's on the chopping block." He shook the can at a thoughtful pace. "Now, let me ask you jizz-bobbers a philosophical question. What if the only woman who couldn't hear you was the one you loved? I mean, what if Mr. Bishop croons like a fucking champ? That's what the Bishops are facing right now. That's what we all face. Sooner or later." He paused. "And in the face of that facing," he said, pointing the can at Abe, "just what the fuck do you think you're doing, Mr. Sullivan? What do *you* know about standards? The only standards that matter are the old standards. And they only matter if you've goddamn well felt enough to belt 'em out. Standing there, Mr. Sullivan, trying to spook some tubby into feeling things *for* you? You know what kind of move that is?"

Schiel cracked the can. Abe closed his eyes and caught the spray all over his face. When the spray stopped he opened his eyes, and Schiel handed him the can. "That's a pussy move," he said. He got up. "So long as you're a pussy, I'm still your fucking coach."

Which might've put our asses in gear, shut things good and tidy, except for that Abe turned and walloped Burk in the back of the head with the can. Bam. This slumped Burk cold, and Schiel had to wrestle Abe onto the floor. They traded blows, Schiel screeching for us to help as Abe jabbed and elbowed, until finally Schiel stiff-armed Abe's forehead and raised the blackout count another kid. Then he left both of them and staggered into the shower area, not even reaching the water knob before he threw up.

෴

When Principal Bernam found me crouched outside his window during his conference with Schiel the next day, he didn't yell. He rested his arms on the sill. "I've been speculating about a sort of anti-video game," he said, squinting down. "In lieu of your typical prostitutes, pistol whipping, etcetera, what I'd like to see invented is a game in which the player controls a desert. The sensitive ecosystem of a desert. The slow, imminent sand."

From behind Bernam came Schiel's laughter, which I reported later as being buttered with disdain and grit. I reported this in Grande Burger, where we huddled minus Abe. He was fine, but his parents were keeping him gowned in the hospital for hype and litigation. Forget about balls: Schiel's ass was roadkill. Even worse, we weren't really sure how we felt.

"Self-defense," Bryan Colby said.

"Whose?" asked Logan Antin.

"Both," Colby said. "Shit, I don't know."

We were in such a clusterfuck of gloom that we didn't eat. Our cap brims were frayed, coaxed and sun-bleached. A few of us wore pooka shells. Anthony Whistler had some kind of ridiculous goddamn cowboy hat. Hunter Limbard's tips were frosted, but it might've been the year for that, you know? Our jeans were baggy, and our T-shirts bore the names of wide receivers and local barbecue sauces. Garth Dole folded a little paper football and flicked it at Logan's face, but nobody even smirked.

I was about to float an "all-Burk's-fault" theory—since he'd escaped spick and span, fat as ever—when Tootie Chavez and Kristina Saiz walked in, fingers in each other's belt loops. Chavez ordered a guacamole burger, Saiz some chili cheese fries. They were tittering and shushing each other, and we watched Saiz pinch Chavez's arm. Her tanktop was black, but her bra straps were definitely yellow.

"Dude," Hunter Limbard whispered.

"Remember when Abe almost had her," Bryan Colby said. "Right in the gym."

Our table was by the soda row, and Chavez nodded when he came over to fill his cup. "How you guys holding together?" he asked, mixing several buttons of soda.

We shrugged.

Chavez laughed and pulled the ice lever. "Man, I've never seen so many dudes on Schiel's jock. Wait, sorry. Half a jock."

We glared. "What about your girlie over there?" I said. "She's getting kicked out of school because of that horse thing."

"Plus," Logan Antin said, yanking his brim low, "she's a slut."

Chavez stopped the ice. He stared at us. Then he grinned. "Hey Krissy," he called.

She looked over, mid-bite into a chili fry. She raised her eyebrows and slurped the fry. Then she wiped a little cheese off her lip.

What's funny about a shit-eating grin is that the grinner's not the eater, or he probably wouldn't be so chipper. So the shit scarfer must be the one getting grinned at. The grin's like, hey, you want some salt with that shit? Too bad. All I got is more shit. Watching Tootie Chavez grin and shrug, we could tell he knew exactly what we tasted.

"Why are you talking to them?" Saiz piped. "They're gross."

"Sorry," Chavez called. "Just some guy talk."

Saiz rolled her eyes. "Ew."

Chavez leaned into our faces, touched his forefinger and thumb together, kissed them, and said "poof," fluttering his hand away like he'd just conjured a butterfly. Then he sauntered over to Saiz. She looked at his cup. "Stupid," she said. "You forgot to get me my iced tea."

"Bitch tea!" yelled Garth Dole, but it didn't make any sense, and his voice kind of broke, and everyone in Grande Burger—taco fryers and yellow bras and even the oft-concussed ex-quarterbacks analyzing x's and o's up on Sportscenter—could turn and see our hearts were low on oomph.

❧

After discovering by way of locked gym doors that night's basketball cancellation (none of us were on the team, though Logan sometimes stripped his shirt in the stands to air an awesome scrawl of red pectoral ink: DIG D33PER DIGGERS!!) we knew we had to find Schiel. We caravanned to his house: big trucks, bigger trucks, Garth Dole's Land Rover, Logan Antin's Mustang and Anthony Whistler's hatchback. Schiel lived in the buttes above the lake, off an old logging road we had to GPS. His house was squat and paneled, red as an old caboose. A generator sat in the front yard. There was a riding lawnmower tipped over on a slope. Ponderosas crowded the house, like hunters poking at something. The roof was smudgy with needles and tar.

Schiel answered the door in a jean jacket and boxer shorts. His hair was scrambled, eyes baggy. He saw most of us standing in his yard, and then he saw all of us. "It's a lynch mob," he said. He coughed and hocked. "Always wondered what that looked like."

"No," Bryan Colby said. "It's to talk."

"Right," Schiel said. "I'm supposed to believe that Abraham Sullivan's guido-ass lawyers come over and assess my TV, my stereo, my tonsils, and then his little cock-swashing friends aren't here to ream me."

"Coach Schiel," I said, licking my lips. "Did Bernam fire you?"

Schiel barked a laugh and scratched himself. "Bernam's afraid of his stove. He's not gonna fire anybody. School board, though. They'll do me in. I'm cooked."

We shoved our hands into the pockets of camo jackets and windbreakers.

"It's cold," Schiel said. "Get inside. There's Keystones in the fridge. I can hardly drink that shit anymore, but you're welcome to it." So we filed into the house, Schiel in the doorway with his arms crossed. "If you're gonna chop me up," he said, "I'd like you to put the pieces in the microwave. Think I'd blow up like a hot dog in there."

For a dude with one ball, he had a pretty sweet pad. Sweet enough, I mean. There were trophies and remote controls. Mustard packets littered like Easter eggs. There was one blanket on his bed and one chair at the kitchen table, an aluminum folding chair, and a fry box full of unopened bills on the table. Kinda sweet, I guess.

We all took a beer and sat with Schiel in the living room. His throne was an old green recliner, and he channel surfed with the TV on mute. Nobody spoke. Schiel stretched his legs, which poked thin and hairy and from his boxers pocked by moles. He had a bottle of Sierra Nevada Pale Ale. We wanted to ask him so much. But we didn't know what. I mean, we snickered when the health teacher said "testicle." Most of what we knew about balls was they hurt when flicked. And something called teabagging, which fags did? For sure was this: here was the dude who'd stressed a gusto of manhood that boiled down to grabbing your cojones and giving the world a smack. But now we'd seen him smacked back, roughed by beast and boy, and we'd discovered that—all along—he may have been reaching down without a full grip.

So we drank. And we watched Schiel's widescreen, muted gags and reruns. When Schiel found an old John Wooden-era UCLA game on ESPN Classic, he waved the controller and said "I was at Hometown Buffet tonight. And I love Hometown Buffet. Bryan, what's your favorite thing at Hometown Buffet?"

"Battered shrimp," said Bryan Colby.

"Breaded shrimp," Schiel corrected. "Anyway, I love it all. Soft serve and corn bread. Some of those mystery ribs. Yam goop! And I like the mirrors. See yourself mirrors. Porn mirrors!" He laughed and pointed at the carpet. "I like gravy the color of that carpet. But listen. What did I eat tonight? Nothing. All the food was gone. Vats full of water. And each of them had, get this, rubber ducks. Like bath ducks. All the heating lamps were on, but only these ducks were bobbing around. Duckies. No food."

We looked at each other. A little bit of eyebrows.

"Was anybody else there?" I asked.

He looked at me like a teacher, waiting for me to answer myself. Somebody humphed, then tried to make it a cough. We felt creeped out. But nobody said shit. For some reason, we felt like if we said anything, he might ask us to explain everything.

"I need to use the bathroom," Anthony Whistler said.

"Number?" asked Schiel.

Whistler ground his jaw. "Two," he admitted.

Schiel went into the kitchen and came back with some coffee filters. "Here," he said.

Right after we heard Whistler flush, Hunter Limbard asked, "What about soda? Was there soda?"

"I don't drink soda," Schiel said. He showed us his teeth. "Do these look like the choppers of a soda guy?"

They were a musky alabaster, like they'd been cured in pickle juice and left on a tanning bed in a basement. For a thousand years, probably. We drained our beer.

Hey, dear gawker, I know what you're thinking. One-balled Schiel with yellow teeth, right? Crazy one-balled Schiel. Getting all wonky in your smirk, probably, just because I told you about the Hometown Buffet thing and I haven't told yet about Schiel shrugging, switching inputs from cable to XBox, and kicking everybody's ass at Madden for the next hour. Flicking the controller with his eyes closed. Burping and ribbing us. We relaxed. We goaded Schiel into old form. He began to wax about women he'd known, aiding his stories with liberal pantomime of tongue, and we weren't ashamed to use the words we knew, words like muff and jizz-map-of-Hawaii. And we took turns, even Anthony Whistler, down at Schiel's bedroom doorjamb, tongue-jocking under the tutelage of a one-balled swami, who towered and hollered, belittling our techniques so thoroughly that we grew rock sure of his love. He loved us so much he feared we'd fail at everything.

But the night. The night was a bitch we couldn't tame. Schiel set pace, and we took the hella-train to sloshland. Soon after Logan Antin knocked himself out by headbutting a box of frozen salisbury, Schiel had us circle around his recliner. "Of this," he said, pointing to the chair, "I do not count myself spatially fond."

The chair was shamrock green, smelled of mothballs and peanut oil. Springs dangled below the seat.

"Let's fuck it up," Garth Dole said.

Hunter Limbard pulled out his Swiss army knife and opened all the tools: screwdriver, nail file, blade.

"Who's got a truck?" Schiel asked. "I want to dump this puppy. Pump this dumpy. I don't know who's sitting on what when I sit in this goddamn thing." He kicked the recliner. It reclined. He jumped on the footrest and the metal twisted, chair snapping into his knee. "Shit," he said, hopping on one foot. Hunter and I grabbed the recliner and carried it outside to Hunter's truck bed. Schiel limped after us. "Sit me down," he said.

"Lemme sit."

A few of us sat in the truck bed with Schiel, asses chilly and awkward. Schiel clutched his armrests. As the truck churned gravel, he lectured us: recipes for beef stew, ways to make glue out of lemon juice, things you should do one-handed. "Memory," Schiel said. "That's the key shit. Every day I mix a little ginseng into my Folgers. I have photographic memory. Ask me a day."

"April twenty-eighth," Bryan Colby said. "Nineteen eighty-six. That's the day I was born."

"Well, son," Schiel said, "Spring of '86. Right. There was a Joshua tree. Some kind of earthquake. I dove into this gap, sort of Earth gap, rescued the ugliest-ass thing. Mongoose, maybe. Some kind of walking catfish."

"Eighteen," Garth Dole said. "Eighteen thousand and eight."

"Space!" Schiel yelled. "I *made* space!"

We asked him where he'd learned to swim. We asked him when he'd started shaving. Then Anthony Whistler asked him what day he got married.

Schiel nodded. "Right," he said. We waited. "Right," he said.

"Like the Polaroids," Anthony Whistler said. "When did you take those?"

"Polaroids?" Schiel said. "They stopped making Polaroids."

Anthony Whistler took out his wallet and mimed throwing it. "No," he said. "Remember? Cum guzzlers? Nudie pics? Something about why something."

Schiel squinted and said nothing. Hunter drove us past an old rollerskate burger place, shuttered, Roo's, now weedy in the parking lot and graffitied on the marquee. We were in the weird part of downtown, like the dustpan. Hairdresser in a boxcar, fake log cabin that called itself the Pioneer Museum, a Victorian with overrun hedges and "BED AND BRAEKEFEST" stenciled onto a prop of driftwood. Nobody hung out around here. These were shortcuts, not streets. We weren't sure where

Schiel wanted to go.

"Is there a Mrs. Schiel?" Anthony Whistler asked. "Was there? Ever?"

I chopped him in the side. He grunted and smacked me.

"You wouldn't get it," Schiel said. "Look at you. Nimrods." He pinched the bridge of his nose and his fingers were trembling. "Cum guzzlers, that's right. That's it. Just shut up, okay? Stop talking."

"You're the one talking," Anthony Whistler said. I went to hit him again but he cracked my face with his elbow—I saw bright. "Your thing," Anthony Whistler said. He smalled himself into a corner of the truck bed. "I'm just saying. You have a thing."

"Let's get to the bridge," Schiel said. "Fuck this. This thing is eating me." He tried to crank his busted footrest, but the lever broke in his hand. He stared at the lever, then chucked it right past our faces, two-seam fastball, and we only knew it hadn't nicked us by how straight it flew.

☙

At the bridge above the river, Schiel supervised our extraction of the recliner, while Anthony Whistler peed off the side and hummed some bumpkin tune. Really the recliner wasn't heavy, but five of us teetered the thing, trying to set it right where Schiel wanted, the pushoff point. "Trust me," Schiel said. "I know the rocks down there. We need a splash. Not a crunch. Splashy splash."

Luckily the hour was such that few headlights passed. But even if somebody might've slowed, braked to gawk at the drunks with their easy chair, there were plenty of little rocks to throw. Plenty of middle fingers. What we liked about the dark was how we clumped. We were swaying with Schiel, and he was swaying with us. We did what he said, balancing for his love, but felt like bros. Bros with Schiel, bros with the night.

Except for Whistler. He had a singing voice that was all nose, which he used to heckle us. "*You're a grand old chair, you're a high flying chair,*" he sang. "*Blah dee dee fuckity blah.*"

"Don't you have a dick to suck?" Bryan Colby snapped.

"Your mom's a dick," Whistler said.

"Men wash their hands," Schiel said, looking at Whistler. "When they shit. Boys take their shit and smear it on their face. How 'bout you clean your face, Mr. Whistler, and let us take care of our little job."

Whistler leered. "I'll shit on your face. I'll shit on your ball."

We all yanked our heads over to Whistler, which caused Hunter Limbard to stumble a little and pull at the recliner for support. He pulled so hard that he pulled the whole thing, and when he bonged against the railing, the recliner toppled onto him. He cursed and heaved the recliner, which tipped over the railing, zoomed into a speck, and hit the river with a pop, splintering across the water like a toothpick castle. Most of the frame sank, but the upholstery snagged on a rock and fluttered there, greenly shining, until it tore into the current.

Bits of frame and metal bobbed. We put our shoes in the bottom rung of the railing and stared. Schiel too, leaning with the best of us. He raked his hair, and stopped with his hand clutching the back of his head, like he was about to scalp himself. "Clean your face," he said, staring at the water. "Take showers. You've got to remember the world doesn't smell like you. If the world smells like anything, it's a candle. One of your mother's goddamn candles."

Anthony Whistler came up behind Schiel and grabbed his wrist. "Show us your rubicon," he said.

Schiel didn't move. "That's a lake in Greece," he said.

"You're not funny," Whistler said. "Show us your fucking cripple ball."

"I'm not trying to be funny," Schiel said. "I'm trying to teach you something."

"You're a gimp," Whistler said. "Another fucking gimp." He pressed his forearm into Schiel's neck.

"Sure," Schiel said. "Say that to my face."

Anthony pushed Schiel into the railing. "Why should I care about your face?"

Below, the river was a shush of blue and shimmer. Night had its shrug on, vast and black. The rest of us? A survey: Hunter Limbard spat in his fingers and started tugging his bangs. Bryan Colby tapped his foot about a million times. Garth Dole pulled up his pants, hobbled a few feet away, and blew chunks in the road. Back at Schiel's place, Logan Antin woke, groaned, pissed in the vegetable drawer of Schiel's fridge, and passed out again. I opened my cell phone, but I couldn't remember how the numbers worked. There were others. Sons and dudes. They've got names. When I see them these days, we greet with our chins.

"Do it," they whispered. "Make him," they said. "Why not?" they said. "Why not."

Whistler kneed Schiel in the crotch and Schiel collapsed. We circled before he could rise. Somebody stomped on Schiel's hands. Somebody else held his ankles. Then Anthony Whistler yanked his boxers. Flopped onto Schiel's thigh, solo, was the ball. Pube curls. Dick, tucked. All the skin had an overfried look. More resting than gimpy. More old than ruined. One old ball at rest.

Schiel had his eyes squeezed and a laugh going. Frozen go-kart laugh.

We all looked at the ball. None of us looked at each other. "Uh huh," Whistler said. "There we go."

☙

The Sullivan family waived all charges. Our guess is Schiel skipped town. We never see him. That summer, Abe hooked up with Saiz, had by all accounts a sweet deal, until he posted these pictures on Facebook of her asleep, naked, boobs spruced with cotton candy. We matriculated. We booed the valedictorian. We booed Bernam, who held up a fake gold nugget during his speech. Garth Dole fought in the UFC until he was looped by coke. Then he drove a cement mixer. He got arrested for trying to fight a cop's motorcycle. Kept stressing he had no beef with the cop. Hunter Limbard started a detail business: rims, chrome, the enchilada. Logan Antin did plenty of waking and looking and falling back asleep. My girlfriend works at the library, and she says that Matt Crane and Tootie Chavez sometimes call to ask if they've got old football tapes. Bryan Colby's a lousy plumber, leaves his wrench in the sink and tries to mooch potato chips. Anthony Whistler plays in a metal band, still with that goddamn cowboy hat. Mud or tussle, he saves the hat. We're doing okay. We're in the process of telling lies and weighing fear. Getting fat and finding girls. Most of what they hear they feel, which is nice. You tell 'em they're in your heart like a flag on the moon, and they touch themselves. Ms. Bishop can't hear anything, of course. She wanders like that. Now and again I'll see her in the supermarket, at the boat ramp, in the bowling alley. What am I supposed to do, learn sign language? Learning's for dick cheese. You want to get by in this world? Then buzz. Keep slick. One of the last things I really cared to learn was this: the Rubicon is a river in Italy. It's where Julius Caesar tipped his hand and kicked Rome into civil ruckus. Bet you thought I didn't know that. Ha. Sucker. Guess that means I'm up on you. Up one and counting.

WHAT THE FUCK IS AN ELECTROLYTE?

Mastodon in a tar pit. Monster truck with a black eye. Nothing Monty could think of got close to how loud he wanted his band. He kept thinking of amps loud enough to rattle sediment. Nu metal that doubled as hydraulic strip mining. Which was funny, that idea, because he'd never even liked nu metal until his brother Tucker hydroplaned on I-80. Black ice and snow had ruined the road, and Tucker slid while barreling west from Reno, a sloppy winner, his car a mess of wine coolers and new fifties. After he lived, people spoke of his luck with their eyebrows aloft, and this pissed Monty off because *people*—who were people?

Tucker's money went to recovery, weeks of drawn shades and soup, as Monty sat Indian-style and played him folk songs. But Tucker banged the nightstand and moaned. Too loud, Monty was too loud. Everything was too loud: commercials, garbage trucks, even rain. One night, a storm clocked an electric pole, and Monty awoke to see a PG&E man in a cherry picker right outside his window. Monty was seventeen. His grades were shit. His father managed a gym and skimmed cash, and his mother guzzled cough syrup until her face drooped. The PG&E man had enormous orange headphones, and he was so close that Monty could make out a Christian fish tattoo on his bicep.

He got up and went into Tucker's room, found Tucker humming rocketship noises. "Dude," Monty said. Tucker kept humming. Monty walked over and punched Tucker's arm. Tucker looked up. He smiled and pointed to his ears. "Tuck," Monty shouted. But Tucker shrugged and fanned his ears, still smiling. With a pen off the nightstand he wrote on his hand: CANT HEAR <u>SHIT!!</u> BOOYAH

When Tucker went deaf, Monty dumped the acoustic. He bought a Gibson SG, black, and started clipping his toenails in the garage. Friends came over late, slouched through the house, polite to Monty's mom on the sofa—*thanks, no* to rooting for white people on reality shows—and polite to Monty's dad with his cast-iron pan—*thanks, no* to fried bologna, fried zucchini. They slunk into the garage, bumped fists with Monty, got high, and traded power chords. It wasn't anything special until Monty got a blowjob from Brooklyn Antoinette Menendez in his dad's Aerostar. Then Brooklyn's sort-of boyfriend Roland broke into Monty's house with a portable drill, stoned and blubbering, and began to stomp and unspool the VHS workout tapes all over the carpet. Monty's dad found him in the dark and kicked his ass, using a coffeepot until the coffeepot broke. To apologize, Monty suggested to Roland that they start a band.

"My fingers are too fat," Roland said.

"Play bass," Monty said. They were drinking Kool-Aid and vodka. Monty kept the garage lit with a flood lamp he'd stolen from the school theatre. Cinnamon incense killed the pot smell. "Bass is cake. A fucking yeti could play bass."

"Is that it?" Roland said. He poured out his Kool-Aid. "Yeti," he whispered. Then he began to cry, cried for a while into his sleeve, hiccups and snot. From the kitchen, Monty could hear the can opener and his parents laughing, drunker than he was. Tucker, he knew, was upstairs playing text-based online role-playing games, growing the rattiest beard Monty had ever seen in living color. All night Tucker clacked away, pausing only to let the modem screech whenever their shitty dial-up booted him. Tucker didn't work, but all he ate was candy. So whatever. When Roland stopped crying, Monty turned on his amp. "Grow a pair," he said.

Two chords and one solo later, they had a song. Monty let Roland do vocals. "Scream until you throw up," he told him. "Except don't throw up."

⌘

They convinced Brooklyn to skip school the next day and listen to their song. Monty's parents weren't home. Roland screamed the song's final line right into Brooklyn's face, but he didn't look at her. All of his body was hunkered into the microphone, clenched and hot, and Monty thought he looked like a jaguar with a head to chew, a muskrat maybe. Whatever jaguars ate to file their teeth. After the last of the feedback drained away, everybody's ears tinning and their heads light, Ronald went to his knees for bombast, and Brooklyn took the microphone. "Calm down," she said. Then Roland bit her wrist and she let him. She craned and gasped a little. "You guys are crazy," she said.

"That was pretty dank," Monty said, watching them.

Roland howled. Brooklyn giggled and pushed him away, sat over on Monty's amp. She dangled her checkerboard Vans. "I couldn't really hear you, but you sounded hella good," she said. "I mean, I could hear you. Just not, like, the words."

Monty nodded. Roland was still on his knees. Monty kicked him in the back, gently. "Be louder, dumb fuck," he said. Roland got up and slung the microphone cord over his neck like a towel. He was bobbing his head. "Fuck yeah," he said. "Fuck yeah."

⌘

They couldn't agree on a name, but they did get this dude Duncan to play drums. Though Duncan was rich and kind of a poser, he had what Monty considered the sickest kit in town. His cymbals were so tall he had to stand a little to crash them. Duncan led them to a name one night after they'd thrashed through a few songs and were feeling pretty pumped. "What about," he said, panting, "Castles of Righteous?"

Roland raised his top lip. "Are you fucking with us?"

"Alright," Duncan said. "Retribution—" he made a fist. "Something. Retribution something."

Tucker walked in. He held a carton of milk. His eyes were mottled and twitchy, and he was wearing unlaced snow boots. His beard dangled to his chest. He dumped the milk on the garage floor and a cockroach skittered away from the puddle.

Monty turned off his amp. He made the sign language for "mom" and "dad" by spreading his right hand and touching his thumb to his chin, then his forehead. Tucker snorted, which sounded like a rat sneeze.

Roland picked his cord off the floor where the milk was spreading. "That's really gross," he said.

"Roach milk," Duncan said. "That's it."

Roland considered. "Nice."

Tucker dropped the carton and walked back inside. Monty stepped over and squished the carton flat. "Roach milk," he said. He pictured the name in large white letters. With a font like eroded stone. Would it make them louder? Loud as fuck? The garage was full of barbells and stationary bikes. His father sometimes cornered him about exercise, about feeling one muscle blend into the next, but Monty didn't give a shit about his muscles. He didn't want to feel himself at all.

"Roach milk sounds gay," he said. "And it's too much like Black Flag."

Duncan kicked his bass drum. "You guys don't even want a name," he said.

"Dude," Roland shrugged. "I liked it."

"How about no fucking name," Monty said. "Nobody Needs a Name."

Duncan and Roland looked at each other. Duncan scratched his head with his drumstick. "That's kind of long. Roach Milk is like—bam."

Monty turned on his amp and played a minor chord. It soaked into the garage. "Whatever," he said. "It's gay, but whatever."

Roach Milk played two shows before they disbanded. At their last show—placing third of four at a YMCA battle of the bands, little kids running to hide in the showers after two songs, but who the fuck let little kids in, Monty wanted to know—Roland found Brooklyn Antoinette Menendez in the parking lot making out in her car with a girl. When he flipped out, they rolled up the window. He beat his knuckles against the glass until they bled, and when he started licking the blood and spitting at the car, Brooklyn peeled away.

Duncan's parents made him sell his kit before college. He didn't even bother offering the drums to Monty. "These or tuition," Duncan told him, sheepish, tossing the kit into his truck bed. Monty thought about chucking a barbell after the truck, but he liked the kit too much to risk it.

Monty didn't go anywhere. After he graduated, he got two jobs: afternoons at the cannery and late-night security at the casino. The owner of his father's gym found out about the embezzling and his father went to jail. At the sentencing, his father unbuttoned the cuffs of his silk dress shirt. Monty's mother was crying and laughing at the same time. "Don't worry," his father said, squeezing her all over. "They're gonna let me wear this in there. It's not even a real jail. Look, they're gonna let me wear this." Monty took one of the tissues out of his mother's purse and tried to shine his boots, but the tissue ripped.

☙

After this, Monty's mother would spend hours spreading peanut butter. Sandwiches, she said. For your father. But she'd put them in the fridge. She made Monty dole her his paychecks, and she never even showed Tucker his disability money. People started coming over with clipboards and ways to take the exercise equipment from the garage. One day a woman came from the internet. Huge in purple sweatpants. She had the weakest voice Monty had ever heard.

"I said is this the Tucker residence," she said.

"The what?" Monty said.

Blushing, the woman asked a third time. "He knows I'm here," she added.

"Tucker doesn't know anybody," Monty said. He filled the doorway so the woman couldn't see his mother asleep on the couch.

"He knows because it's three o'clock," the woman said. Her face was bleach-pale, and she kept running a thumb above her lip.

Monty heard something lumping downstairs and turned to see Tucker dragging their father's biggest duffel bag. Tucker's beard hung to his thighs, and Monty could see a Q-Tip in the scrag.

This is Audrey, Tucker signed. He smiled at Audrey, who blushed again. She made the sign for the verb instead of his name. Tucker made a laugh sound.

"Give me a break," Monty said. He could feel his chest ripple, and he tried to stop himself from breathing too much.

Don't worry, Tucker signed.

"We met on Marradon," Audrey said. "It's a game world."

You know I need this, Tucker signed to Monty. He repeated the sign for *need.*

Monty didn't help them carry anything, but Tucker didn't have a lot to carry. Audrey's car was a Mini Cooper, yellow-roofed with racing stripes. Monty watched Tucker lug his computer to Audrey's trunk, the tower then the monitor, cords snaking through the grass, catching on sprinkler heads. Monty's mother slept with her lips parted, cushion between her legs. When Audrey started the car, Monty saw Tucker pull her t-shirt at the shoulder and kiss that skin.

❧

Monty's mother vacuumed Tucker's room then bolted the door. "Best sell that Aerostar," she said. Monty printed flyers and stapled them on phone poles. People called and inspected, hemmed and hawed, kicked the fender and stuck their fists in the exhaust pipe. Finally, the tennis coach from Monty's old high school wrote a check. "The district's supposed to cover this shit," he said. He shrugged and bit a banana. He and Monty were at the kitchen table with paperwork. Monty put the pink slip in a manila folder and wrote the date, feeling like he was taking an exam. The coach wore plaid shorts and wraparound sunglasses.

"Asians," he said, scratching under his eye. "Team's full of Asians. Ting starts playing and wham: cousin Tong's gotta scoop the action. Pretty soon you've got enough Asians out there to make some sort of xylophone. Ping pong sching schong. But God bless 'em. They can volley. Can't serve, but sure as shit can they volley. Now it's like, where am I gonna put them all? Well, bingo. My boy Mr. Aerostar to the rescue." He held up his hand for a high five.

Monty rose and opened the refrigerator, got a tea jar of Kool-Aid. "You want some?" he said.

The coach scoffed. "If you're gonna down that sugar water, get it with electrolytes."

"Electrolytes," Monty said, pouring. He thought about how many times he'd heard people say that word. People after people. Making goals and guzzling electrolytes. What the fuck is an electrolyte, he thought. Sure they sound impressive, like they glow and you should look them up, fill your life with them. But why? How much could they really help?

Monty's mother walked in. She wore a wrinkled pantsuit. Her cheeks had little smears of unabsorbed cold cream. Before Monty could stop her, she hugged him. "If I didn't have the sun," she said. "If I didn't have either one of my beautiful afternoon suns!" She winked at the coach. "S-o-n," she said. "You our van man?"

"Proudly," the coach said. He waved his banana at Monty's mother.

"For my tennis team."

"Tennis!" Monty's mother shouted. "There's something I miss. Barely enough time to sneak away from the desk and make lunch with my boy." She jiggled Monty's shoulder. "I remember when they put Jimmy Connor on the Wheaties box—you know what I did? I called the hotline and asked for five more!"

The coach grinned: mouth lopsided, eyes tinted by glass.

Monty poured Kool-Aid and didn't stop. The Kool-Aid overflowed the glass and pooled red across the counter. He kept pouring. Whole tea jar of the shit, he figured. His mother didn't notice until a puddle reached her feet. She shrieked. "Where's the sponge?" she yelled. "Don't hide the sponge."

The coach swiped his manila folder and held it to his chest.

When he'd emptied the whole jar, Monty stuck his thumb in the spill and tasted the Kool-Aid. No electrolytes.

❧

Now Monty had to walk. The cannery wasn't too far from his house, but getting to the casino was a bitch. Buses didn't run that late, so he was stuck with a good couple miles of legwork. In the summer, he tied his t-shirt around his waist. Even early, the heat felt like somebody composting molten chalk all over his body. He sweated and scowled, passing ranch houses and check-cashing places, abandoned laundromats and imported palm trees. There was Thai food in an old Long John Silvers, knickknacks in converted saloons. Shacks that sold pemmican, tackle, and dreamcatchers. Signs about cigarette prices, assholes making wide turns in their R/Vs. Once he saw an old Indian on a mountain bike, wearing a studded cowboy hat and hauling a rickshaw full of canned yams. Twice he saw cop cars outside the bowling alley, which opened to serve beer after bars closed. And that's where he saw the burn welts on the right foot of

Brooklyn Antoinette Menendez.

She was seated outside, yakking at a cop. Her hair was bleached in a way Monty didn't remember. She was showing the cop her foot when she noticed Monty. After the cop walked away to talk into his shoulder, Brooklyn limped across the parking lot. "Fucking gravel," she said.

"The hell you do to yourself?"

Her welts were bright maroon and crusty. In the early light they seemed to glitter, but Monty knew that was just from walking where the cars parked.

"I tried to karate a guy," Brooklyn said. "But he grabbed and put his lighter all over my damn foot. Trick, he calls it. Jesus."

"You drunk?"

She blew on the hair above her eyes. "Let's book before I get my ID back."

"Sick of your birthday?"

Brooklyn grabbed his arm and tugged him into walking. She grimaced and gingered her foot. "It's a fake ID, dumbass."

Then the cop whistled at them, and Brooklyn ran. Ha, Monty thought. He took after. His waist shirt came loose. They cut through backyards. Monty saw a dog and swerved, but the dog was asleep. Monty kept glancing at Brooklyn, who had her teeth crunched. "It's good," she kept saying. "It's good. I can't feel it." In a yard with a kiddie pool, Brooklyn stopped and dumped herself ass-first on the lawn. She coughed and spit while Monty squished his shoe into the pool. It was empty.

"Was he even chasing us?" he said.

"Exercise," Brooklyn panted. "Keep my figure with this shit."

Monty lay down and felt the grass tickle his ear. "I'm supposed to be sleeping right now," he said.

"Fuck that. Buy me a doughnut."

"I hate doughnuts."

"Buy me a creamsicle, then." She sighed. "Go for broke."

Monty put his face in the grass and chewed. Brooklyn came over and sat on his ankles. She weaved her nails down his back, put her fingers under his belt. "It's rush hour," she said.

ↄ

When Monty told his mother he was crashing from now on with Brooklyn Antoinette Menendez, she smirked, watched an episode of Judge Judy, then locked herself in the bathroom. "Can't take the guitar," she said. "Your father paid for that guitar."

"Yeah?" Monty called. He brought his guitar case to the bathroom door, peeled stickers off and stuck them on the wood. "Can I get some weekend visits?"

"Smart-ass. Top of everything else, I've got a smart-ass."

Monty left the case and went into his room. He tore the sheets off his mattress, dragged the mattress off his bed, carried it to the bathroom and propped it against the door. Every window in the house was open; his mother wouldn't run the swamp cooler. Fruit flies had command of one kitchen corner and were jonesing for others. Most of the garage shit had been gutted—liquidated, his mother said. Weekends the tennis coach visited, brought mojito mix and packaged food kits: taco kits, sushi kits. Weekdays his mother would munch taco shells. Mostly all she wore was a sweatsuit and an unknotted tie.

In high school, Monty knew a pediatrician's son. Rich douche. After junior prom, Monty somehow ended up on this son's trampoline with a bunch of other kids. When they wanted to go inside and drink, the son got pissed and made everybody split. Later, Monty found out that the pediatrician liked to unwind by mopping naked. Monty wanted to call the son, but he knew he'd get an answering machine. He wanted to uncork a tide of guitar feedback that would melt that answering machine before it could even fucking beep.

His mother began to cuss. She flushed the toilet and cussed louder. "There's shit in my blood," she yelled. "You cock-ass faggot shitheads. There's blood in my fucking shit. Is that happy? Are you pleased?"

Monty got a steak knife. He cut holes in the mattress. Then he shoved the mattress over and beat the door until his mother opened up. She looked at the knife. Her pants were down and her face seemed precarious, poorly stacked. She turned her back to Monty, craned out the window and beckoned air. "See what you goddamn faggots all do for me."

Monty tossed the knife into the sink. He looked at the toilet bowl. There was a good amount of blood, but no shit. Strands of blood, floating all by themselves.

❧

Roach Milk reunited a little when Monty had to throw Duncan out of the casino. Out of the Bow & Arrow Lounge, specifically. Duncan was trying to sell marijuana to two soldiers during a funk concert. The soldiers—drunk and buzz-haired, with dog tags and girls they kept mixing up—tried to kick Duncan's ass. Monty didn't want to fight the soldiers, so he joined them. All the commotion fizzled the music, except for the bass player, who wore enormous purple sunglasses shaped like elephants: he slapped and swayed, oblivious. Finally, the girls pulled the soldiers off Duncan. One of the girls spilled one of the soldier's beers; the soldier lifted his shirt and made her lick his abs.

After the funk resumed, Monty dragged Duncan to the men's room. The music was muffled, but a loose faucet buzzed from the bass. Someone had dragged a ream of paper towels across the sinks. One of the urinals hung at a tilt. ~~GET FUKD~~ *GIT FUCKED* was Sharpied on the mirror. Duncan had cuts on his face and kept squeezing his dreadlocks. "My brain's leaking," he slurred. Droopy-eyed, he stared at himself and Monty in the mirror. "Yo, you were in my band."

Monty sat in the skewed urinal. "Hurry up," he said. "I have to throw you out."

But Duncan was beaming and snapping his fingers. He smacked the mirror. "You were in Roach Milk!" he said. "Monty something. Man, those were the sweet days, right? Those were the Little Debbie days, motherfucker." He reached out his hand to Monty, who hesitated, then slapped Duncan's palm. Their fingers slid and locked, boomeranged apart. Monty flexed his fist, which hurt from punching Duncan, and Duncan kept flopping his hand like he was drying it. Monty sat in the urinal and watched as Duncan began to do some ridiculous hippie dance, shoulders bobbing, spaced-out grin. "It wasn't your band," Monty said. "Where the fuck did you go, anyway?"

"Humboldt State," Duncan said. "I been resting with the fern gullies. Doing that yah mahn. I been log-dogging that outlook of progress, you feel me? Shit's all in the woods." Still dancing, he took a baggie out of his pocket and shook buds and stems all over his hair.

"You went to Humboldt State," Monty said. "Then you came back here."

"Went is the modus of operation," Duncan said. "I dropped that shit like a seaside sunset. Three years in the State, man. Three years in the skeptical of the Boss Brother. It's all simulacrum and faso-sadism." He ripped a scrap of paper towel and daubed his face. "This shit's made from organisms, yo."

"Where did you sell your kit?" Monty said.

"Kit-Kat?"

"Your drums."

Duncan laughed. "Truth bomb! That's the kinda truth a State tries to gum up, you know? Fuck the State, man. Fuck that fascist university shit. Fast and be universal, you know?"

Monty felt the urinal below his ass, a dampness, but he knew that nobody would see a stain in the dark. Nobody would be staring at his ass.

Not with the strobe lights, the Chesterfields and wads of dip. Not with the droops of belly fat, the shark tooth necklaces, the chinstrap beards and tacky mascara, all of the people in the dark with their paper wristbands, cover paid and eyes red, scanning for the hottest, shiniest, and most susceptible, hoping and dreading to see the whole goddamn town. Monty knew that nobody would notice him. Not until somebody flipped out and he had to collar them. *Fuck this shit,* they'd bellow. And Monty knew of the shit they meant, he understood why they were always trying to fuck that shit, but all they ever did was fuck themselves. Shit, meanwhile, kept thumping away, pervasive as the bass that people—who called and complained—could hear for miles. But nobody—not the cocksuckers in the casino, not the squares dinking around in the foothills—would care about his wet ass. Why should they? Who did anything worth caring about? People hawked their drums. They wore orange headphones. Purple sweatpants. They played text-based RPGs. They mopped naked. Without permission or proof, they accused others of luck. They sought electrolytes as welts glittered and roaches crawled from milk. Roach milk. Monty still hated the name, but at least Duncan had remembered. Most people, Monty thought, they didn't even fill their fucking kiddie pools.

Duncan danced slower and slower, crouched and passed out. Monty got up and dug in Duncan's pockets, found a wallet and baggies of shake. He took the shake and tossed Duncan's wallet on a bed of paper towels. Monty knew he'd probably see him that weekend in Taco Bell, churro dust on his fingers. He wondered if he was living with his parents. If they'd make him lose the dreadlocks. Monty grabbed Duncan's limp hand and tore off his wristband.

☙

After the concert, the bass player from the funk band strolled over to Monty. He was still sporting his elephant sunglasses. But Monty looked and saw they were hollow. His shirt was silk and open-throated, pockets scalloped. He punched Monty in the chest. "Damn son," he said. "You kept a handle out there. We're grateful as hell. You want the tour?"

The band's bus had black carpet and cup holders that glowed. One dude was eating a TV dinner and popping antacids. Another had a straw in a bottle of wine. A woman in a kimono sat on the floor, whispering into a cell phone and hiding her mouth with her hand. Several table fans swiveled and whined, and the bus smelled of ammonia and coffee. When Monty and the bass player walked in, all the guys grunted cheers, but the woman kept whispering.

Monty sat while the bass player ducked into the back. The woman snapped her cell phone shut and glared at him. "Podunk fucks," she said.

"Podunk funk!" somebody said, and the band laughed.

"This a living for you?" she asked Monty. "What are you, one-eighth?"

Somebody leaned over to Monty. The drummer, maybe. "Nobody pays," he said. "Jews, Indians, crackers, don't matter. Nobody pays. You know who I am?" Monty stared at him. "Neither do I," the guy said.

"I'm not tribal," Monty said.

The woman looked at her phone. "That wasn't even a business call." She lay back on the floor and set a pillow on her face.

The bass player returned in a robe, still with the sunglasses. He carried a gold vinyl record. "John Hancocks," he shouted. "Finger, set, go."

"Aw, c'mon," somebody said. "Give him a real CD."

The drummer got up and opened a mini fridge. He tossed something to Monty: a package of thin-sliced deli ham. "Don't get a stomachache," the drummer said.

"What do you go by?" asked the bass player. He had the record smooshed against the wall, a marker in his mouth, elephants sliding down his nose. Just then, the bus sputtered and revved. The bass player stumbled, but he kept a hold on the record, clamped his teeth on the marker.

Monty thought awhile. "Tucker. Make it out to Tucker."

"With a T?"

Monty nodded.

"Seriously," somebody said.

"Fuck off," said the bass player. "Tucker, listen, you want a real CD?"

Monty shook his head. He stared at the ham. "Whatever you got," he said.

"See?" said the bass player. "Here's a kid who knows up from up." He signed the gold vinyl meticulously, swoops in slow motion. Monty watched out the window as the bus reversed in the casino parking lot, honking and blinking. From the floor, her voice half-smothered by the pillow, the woman began to hum one of the band's songs.

LOOK! LOOK! FEATHERS

Same Heart They Put You In

More you know Marianne, the more you care what she likes. Right now she's up shotgun, cheek scrunched against the window, the sleeves of her Mickey Mouse sweater drooping over her hands. Wine country slopes by, green and buzz cut vineyards, gobs of lazy hill. Cheri drives. I'm in the seat behind her. The sun's drifting up. Everything is olive oil, a spilled yawn. We're headed back to Oakland after this weird birthday party at a villa. Dude named Graham. There was gin, Mexican milk cake, kitschy Star Wars action figures. We're at that age where the sighs get less and less fake. It's because of Marianne's effect on the world that I'm not behind her, massaging her neck or something. We let her sleep. Cheri and I know each other only because of her.

"Do you think Graham had fun?" Cheri whispers.

"Sure," I say. "He was really nice."

"He loves Marianne."

"It seems like he's a really expressive guy. Why wouldn't he have fun?"

Cheri lets go of the steering wheel for a second. "It's a long story."

"I love Graham," Marianne mumbles. "It might be I'll always love him, I think."

If I want, the backseat is big enough to sleep full stretch. Hours of wine country. Full stretch.

"Graham's mom split when Graham was like, four," Cheri says. "Big Graham took him and moved in with Jacqui. They don't like us anymore. His friends, I mean. They don't like his friends anymore."

To go to the bathroom at the party, you had to get Graham's girlfriend Beth to walk you through the house. Big Graham and Jacqui were on the couch smoking cloves. A flat-screen TV played the Weather Channel on mute. In the room was a pewter statue of a frog and a grandfather clock. Big Graham had a flannel coat. He was gaunt, his beard a spider web. Jacqui wore a white golf cardigan, wool, and a series of bracelets that jangled on his arm in glow stick colors. He gaped a smile at us. Big Graham said, "Fun's a pretty noisy fun, Bethany?" His voice had a weird coo that didn't agree with his look. Beth sat down with them. She pointed up the stairs. At the top of the stairs was a baby gate I had to step over. In the bathroom, a huge tube of Crest lay in the sink, uncapped. The toilet had an auto-flush. There were no towels anywhere. Downstairs, Beth had a clove of her own. They all had their heads close, voices going. But I couldn't hear what anybody said. When they saw me, Beth said, "You're all set." She seemed tired. She handed her clove to Jacqui. Big Graham leaned forward and watched us leave.

Once or twice that night I saw Jacqui outside. Never with Big Graham. Instead he had this gangly teenaged boy, Mexican-looking. I didn't see the boy in the house. They just threaded around, those two—didn't party with us. Jacqui did his smile thing. The party stayed in the courtyard. Card tables and lawn chairs were scattered around the iron fountain. People munched and made nerdy jokes. I didn't know anybody, but I knew nerdy jokes, so I felt okay.

Me and Marianne, we're friends on the internet. When we first met in person, I made a joke about skeeball, and she seemed to like it. That same night, we ended up making out and getting each other off. The next morning we held hands a little, walking to catch my BART for the airport. These days we talk on the IM, especially when we're home and drinking solo. Once or twice a year, I visit.

Cheri's her housemate and Graham's their buddy. At the party, he was still wearing his work duds: black button-down, ironed chinos. He had long hair and glasses. Seemed really excited by each of his birthday presents. Even by all the food. And each friend, like he hadn't expected them to show. "Marianne!" he said when the three of us walked up. "Marianne! Cheri!" He hugged everybody like he'd just invented their faces. I liked him. He gave some basic vibes of coziness to a pretty weird scene. Like on the way to the party, Cheri told us that Big Graham would bring the guard dogs when we parked, which he did.

Meanwhile, here comes dawn.

"If I tell you about this," Cheri says, "You can't spread it."

"Does Marianne know?"

"Lots of people know. It was in the papers and stuff. It's just—it's better if it gets less known instead of more, you know? Marianne knows. You know, Marianne?"

Marianne breathes.

"She's asleep," Cheri says.

"I don't think she's asleep," I say.

Cheri drives for a while. "It's not that you know anybody who could hurt him," she says. "It's not that, exactly."

❧

When Graham's mom left, Cheri tells me, they were living on a houseboat down the coast. Big Graham was working for the Navy as some kind of radio operator. Antennas pointed at the Pacific. Maybe it wasn't the Navy, Cheri says. But something government. This was Reagan '80s. Even people like Big Graham were getting their shit together. He'd met Graham's mom, eased off the mescaline, ditched Orange County, and delved into a little dream of houseboat life. But things'll be things. And all things being so, Graham's mom split, and Big Graham started to cuss at his bosses. Started keeping his own logbook alongside the official one, a yellow secret. One day, he brought a dead seagull aboard the houseboat. He rested the seagull on the kitchen table. Then Little Graham watched as his father sawed the seagull open with a steak knife and began to scoop entrails and bones, arranging them in wet glops on the table, in pentagrams and crescents. When Big Graham noticed his son watching, he stopped. Wiped his hands on his shirt. They been tinkered up for something, he said. We've got to get them set back.

Soon Big Graham was fired. Maybe court-martialed, Cheri says. Anyway, they had to leave the houseboat in the middle of the night and drive up to Napa County, up to Jacqui's villa.

Jacqui didn't make his money in wine. First he sold drugs in L.A, then in the mid '70s he got a bead on an abandoned hot springs site near St. Helena. He bought it and spiffed up the services quite a bit. Opened marijuana saunas, happy endings all over the place. You could add discharge to your baths like ice cream toppings: bull semen, lynx sweat. And, as a good ex-dealer, he kept things hush, which people appreciated. Hollywood types walked around in full dangle. Blow came in salt shakers. Jacqui made so much money that he bought out the other hot springs in the area. Solid knack for business, that guy. We don't know where he's from or anything, Cheri says, but we've never seen that guy want for much. His favorite thing was to hire wincing teenagers, sad sacks drifting to or from the Bay. He'd put those boys in towels and their eyes on ice. Acid blots and prime rib is what he fed them. And what can you say? They got jobs and anything they mentioned. Lush days in a place that pretty much trademarks its light. Jacqui loved to be thanked, that's all. Who doesn't love to be thanked?

"Big Graham was a pool boy?" I say.

"I'm getting the order mixed up," Cheri says. "They met in L.A. Before Jacqui's empire. They knew each other in drugs, I think."

"Thanks," Marianne says. "Thanks. No, thank you. Thank you."

I can't tell if she's dreaming or joking.

"Nobody doesn't," I say to Cheri. "Everybody likes to thank people."

"Exactly," Cheri says. She sighs.

When Big Graham showed up on Jacqui's doorstep with a runt in tow, it was a bigger case of charity than Jacqui was used to. But he let them move into the main house. Wonder what that was like, Cheri says. Those three in the night. Little Graham puffed in a parka maybe, though it wasn't cold. Big Graham shivering and making his case. Jacqui, a lot shorter than Big Graham, probably wore some kind of necklace. Chest hair and gold. Maybe the house was full of boyfriends. Jacqui used to have one boyfriend, Cheri says, who dressed only in oversized jerseys and lived in the water tower. Probably Jacqui didn't think to shoo them all, so Little and Big Graham strolled in and had to step over some boy sleeping on the shag. Jacqui told Little Graham to watch TV, but Big Graham said he wasn't allowed. So all three of them sat at the kitchen counter on barstools. Porcelain toaster. One of those fake little trees to keep bananas fresh. Jacqui made some cocoa with mint schnapps. He guzzled; Big Graham sipped. Little Graham drank too fast and burned his mouth, but nobody noticed. Jacqui asked about timelines. Practicalities. Big Graham said they just needed a safe place to sort things out. That they were crawling, basically, under a major network, and he needed to go deeper. He couldn't exactly communicate through, he said, and he made a motion to his lips and ears. Then he asked Jacqui if he had a pen, and Jacqui found a highlighter in a drawer. Big Graham got a paper towel and wrote on it with the highlighter. Big Graham sank down. He stroked Jacqui's ankles. He began to weep. Jacqui put his necklace in his mouth. Stared at Little Graham, who must have just sat there on his barstool and swiveled. God, Cheri says. What do you think when you don't know any better? Before you start to size up other lives and go *wait*? Growing up in that house, driving spaceships through the shag carpet, waving your hand in front of the toilet to flush it, pretending you're a toilet wizard. Playing Monopoly with shirtless and strung-out young men. And then, not knowing any better, you bring a friend home.

"There's no such thing as weird," I say. "Life isn't, like—" and then I make a straight arrow motion with my hand.

"Don't listen to him," Marianne mumbles. "He's just being intellectual."

I stare at her and snort. I scoot over in the backseat and push her headrest. "*Your letters all say that you're beside me now,*" I sing. "*So why do I feel alone?*"

"I'm trying to sleep," she says.

We drive. We swoop and curve. Cheri turns and looks at me. She has a chubby '50s pin-up look. "She likes you," she says. "She's told me."

"Sleep," Marianne says. "Is one of the most important things in a real person."

I lie down in the backseat. "What's the big thing? What's the bad shit?"

They got domestic, Cheri says. Big Graham made all the meals. He fried things and wandered around in a bathrobe, half-loaded pistol in his monogrammed pocket. Jacqui took Little Graham shopping for pencils and sweaters, and Big Graham waited for the meter reader to leave, then scoured the meters for new wires. He got down on his knees to lick the ruts left in the driveway by the meter reader's tires. Jacqui enrolled Little Graham in a swanky private school and wore skinny red ties to parent-teacher conferences. He gave him very careful haircuts. Jacqui's boyfriends liked the kid, but not Big Graham, who would sneak around and take notes on things—light sockets, fan blades—that didn't need notes. Instead of sleeping he seemed to just glare. So Jacqui had to slip off to his guest houses for his blowjobs or whatever.

"Did he ever—" I say, and Cheri shakes her head.

"If he'd ever touched Little Graham—" she says. She puts her hand on her face. "Big Graham would've taken his face, like this, and after he was done tearing he would've taken what was left and ran it through the garbage disposal."

"What about him and Jacqui? Do they sleep together?"

"They must, right?"

I think on that.

Marianne is looking out the window.

Jacqui bought Little Graham all the toys he saw on TV, Cheri says. He watched Little Graham play, and whenever Little Graham pretended a toy into something else, called Batman a wrestler, Jacqui would go out and buy a toy wrestler, the real version of the something else. Sometimes Big Graham saw Little Graham playing with some toy he didn't like' and threw a fit. Once, he took Little Graham's Ghostbusters car and set it on fire. Then he put the melted plastic in the bathtub and told Little Graham to take a shower.

"Jesus," I say.

"That's the amazing thing," Cheri says. "Little Graham is one of the sweetest kids I know. The sweetest."

They met, Cheri says, in fifth grade. Big Graham read something in the paper about a guest speaker at Graham's old school and made Jacqui switch him. He came to the new school in a black and green t-shirt that said VEGAS, BABY! The teacher sat him next to me, Cheri says, and I watched him draw what looked like Super Mario levels all over his notebook. I was such a nerd, Cheri says. All I did was play video games and listen to my dad's prog rock records. So this kid was the coolest fucking kid ever. At lunch the first day, me and my other nerdy friends sat by Graham. He opened his lunchbox and took out a baggie of olives. Each with a different color or filling. Very shyly, he asked if anyone liked boursin cheese. What's that? somebody said. He gave him the boursin cheese olive. We all waited while the kid nibbled the olive. It's kind of like cream cheese, he said finally. After that, Graham always had somewhere to sit.

You know when you run into somebody you were a kid with, and you don't have much to talk about but going to school together? So you start talking, like, remember Lonnie? How he'd go around at recess picking up acorns and giving them to girls? And you guys start to laugh, trying to one-up each other at Lonnie memories? Well, we were the Lonnies, Cheri says. We knew the right answer, but we'd rather write 80085 on our calculators. We watched MTV and wore blue lipstick. We listened to punk rock before it was in the mall. We farted when the DARE officer got to the solemn part of his speech. Things we discussed included joke elaboration and hot tub sex. Off limits were sports and—usually—what our homes felt like. The older we got, the more time we spent near the railroad bridge, chugging whatever liquor the night grudged up.

"I'm going kind of slow," Cheri says.

"It's fine," I say, thinking how I'll gussy things when I write it all down.

"I should tell you about the first time I saw his house."

Big Graham never let Graham play at anybody else's, she says. And he didn't allow guests. Jacqui would always pick Graham up right after school in his little vintage MG. But for Little Graham's thirteenth birthday, Jacqui convinced Big Graham to let him throw a party. We still measure "hella sweet" by that party, Cheri says. There was a make-your-own sundae bar. Water bazookas. Music we actually liked at volumes never allowed us. And Little Graham was really giddy, not shy like at school. He ran around the whole day sharing presents, screaming louder than anybody. We'd only bought him scrawny Sex Pistols bandannas and stuff, but Jacqui complimented everybody, which made us feel better. The only thing we couldn't do was go inside the house.

"Ah," I say. "Except to use the bathroom."

"Nope," Cheri says. "There was this weird stone outhouse. It was great, actually. We thought it was funny, like a funny camp."

"Where was Big Graham?"

Late in the party, Cheri says, Little Graham pulled me aside and asked if I wanted to see his Nintendo. Well, of course I did. So we went in. Big Graham was on the couch in his bathrobe, and his beard was longer then. Like past his neck. Next to him was one of Jacqui's boy toys, except I didn't know that. He was just this older kid in cutoff jean shorts and a Yankees hat. They were smoking a joint. The room was crammed with things that looked too clean or expensive to touch. Big Graham had an erection; that's something I noticed. And the two Rottweilers at his feet, who sat up when we entered. They barked.

This is my dad, Little Graham said.

Easy now, Big Graham said to the dogs.

Well, I was fucking punk rock, right? So I went over to those dogs and crouched and smiled. They quivered. I went "Shh" and reached to pet them, but Big Graham yanked them back. They barked right at me. Vampire teeth and jowl drool. I flinched, and I could see Big Graham flex his knuckles as he held their scruff.

They like to eat garlic, Yankees Cap said. They love a little thing of garlic.

His voice was like a bored history teacher's.

Big Graham scratched the dogs. Is it that time of year? he said.

This is the Cheri I told you about, Little Graham said. We're just gonna play some Nintendo in my room.

There was this weird pause. And I remember the joint smoke smelled strange, fermented or something.

Then Big Graham asked us a question: Do you need, he said slowly, to use the television console?

I can plug it in for you, Yankees said.

We're all set, Little Graham said.

I've been to Hawaii, Big Graham said. It was a long time ago, but I've been there.

Yankees sighed. Succulent, he said.

Big Graham crossed his legs, kept ahold of the dogs. He stared at me. He said, Cheri, let me tell you about Hawaii.

Dad, Little Graham said. We're supposed to play Nintendo.

Nintendo, Big Graham said. Let me say one thing about Nintendo. I have slept on a beach. With my mouth. In the sand. I have had krill swim into my fucking mouth. I have had fucking *krill* swim into my motherfucking *mouth*. Nintendo! I have slept three feet away from the *sun*. That piece of shit, Jesus-sucking sun. Nintendo! Listen, I have gone back and forth with the same goddamn heart they put me in. He shook his head. The dogs quivered. Nintendo, he said.

His robe fell open a little. I could see rib bones and hair. I was thirteen. I looked for his cock. But there was too much hair to be sure.

Yankees said, There's pineapple soup in Hawaii.

The Rottweilers had the faces of old miners, except for those tongues. Long tongues. And the teeth. You could see the bones in Big Graham's hands as he gripped the dogs. The room had that kind of light where you can't tell the time.

Big Graham leaned back and closed his eyes. Three feet, he said.

Thanks, Little Graham whispered. Thanks, Dad.

☙

We're on the freeway now. Early morning Bay Area drivers, swerving lanes with lattes on their knees. It's June, and the air conditioner is going full blast. Marianne snores. Cheri doesn't bother with her turn signal.

"I haven't told you about the lip," Cheri says. "I'm sorry that it's going like this, but if I'm going to tell you about the lip, I had to tell you about everything else."

"Don't be sorry," I say.

"Ha."

We got older, Cheri says. Life was feeling more arbitrary, annoying, embarrassing. Little Graham was getting old as the boys in Jacqui's harem. He grew his hair. Begged us to help him sneak out to parties. But even though we wanted to skullfuck the State, we were scared to shit of Big Graham. And Jacqui too, who seemed too weak to defy him.

First, Graham didn't like grunge. We showed him Eddie Vedder and he crossed his arms. That's not the right kind of yelling, he said. He started to wear black tank tops and listen to weird metal. European stuff. We couldn't really call him Little Graham after he started working out. Don't get me wrong, Cheri says. He was still a sweet kid. Quickest to laugh and always up with Star Wars trivia. But he started to drip a little edge. Right when we were smoking pot, listening to guitar feedback and getting revelatory about boredom, he would shrug. I wish I felt bored, he'd say.

High school's a friend buffet, Cheri says. That's true. But Graham was starting to hang out with the same kids who tried to elbow us in P.E. Not the cool kids. Cool kids watched us get beat up and didn't really care. But the beaters, Graham started sulking around with them. The dumb fuck Limp Bizkit-listening beaters. Boys who poked their little brothers in the eye with KFC chicken bones when their mom wasn't looking.

"You mean poor kids," I say.

"Look, my mom's a hairdresser," Cheri says. "And my dad, who knows? There's poor then there's mean. Can we agree on that?"

Marianne has terrific hair. Morning slides around in her hair.

"You're like her," Cheri says. "You're quick to guess at things."

"And be wrong?"

"And be wrong."

One night, Cheri says, Jacqui called her on the phone. He was freaking out. He'd gone into Graham's room to ask him to turn down his stereo, but Graham was gone. So he let the stereo go and went downstairs. He told Big Graham dinner was his treat tonight. Then he made a huge pot of spaghetti and tranquilizers. Big Graham conked out. Jacqui and his boys looked all over the villa for Graham, but they couldn't find him. Please, Jacqui said. You're a calm girl, Cheri. That's what he said. You're a calm girl. You're good to him. Please help.

I started calling my friends, Cheri says. Found out about a party at an apartment complex on Old Vine Way. I went. The apartments were that single story motel-type. In the parking lot were three little boys. Two held a string of lit Christmas lights at either end, like a jump rope. One had a ball-peen hammer and a blindfold. He was trying for the lights. Somebody came out of an apartment with his shirt off, jeans sagging, plaid boxers. He cocked his head at me. Where's the pizza, he said.

I'm not the pizza lady, I said.

Damn, bitch, he said. Just messing.

Is Graham in there?

Free country, he said.

Inside, nu metal blared. People sat around on beanbag chairs. A yellowish mattress lay on the floor. Everybody had a forty. One girl took a beanie off a boy's head and stuffed it down her shirt. The living room blended into the kitchen, one of those arrangements where the kitchen counter looks like a teller window. A half-crumpled packet of beef jerky sat on the TV, which was almost bigger than the mattress. There was a smell of fresh paint. Bud cans in the microwave, Bud Lite cans in the sink. This dude with chin scraggle grabbed my elbow. His face was vague. You got a camera, he asked. I need somebody to get this, he said. Then he made some weird shapes with his fingers.

In the bathroom, I found a girl sitting in the shower—there was a handicap bench—with some guy's face in her crotch. She had her arms up, clutching the showerhead, strangling it.

Graham was in one of the bedrooms, wearing an Oakland Raiders jacket a few sizes too big. He squealed when he saw me, gave me a hug. He was hella baked. Fuck fuck fuck fuck, he kept saying, grinning the whole time.

I feel weird about this, I said, but I think I'm rescuing you.

I love that movie, Graham said.

I put my hand in his, but he pulled me over by a closet. There were other people in the room, but I don't think I'll ever know their names. Graham kissed me. He kissed my neck and my hands and my lips, Cheri says.

"That's exact," I say.

Cheri nods. "He was exact about it."

I told him we had to ditch, Cheri says. I told him Big Graham was gonna be pissed as shit.

He pawed his hands on my face like a blind person. I'm gonna piss on *his* fucking shit, he said.

I whispered his name a few times, trying to move him. Finally, sort of waltzing, we got back to the living room. One of the couch's arms was ripped. Graham grabbed some of its stuffing and put it in my hair. Then the guy from the finger shapes showed up. He started going off about how Graham hadn't put in for the keg. I remember asking him what keg? There was no keg. But Graham started screaming at the dude. He went, You're a fucking keg. You're a fucking keg. Then Finger Shapes yanked my arm and Graham flipped out. He started to windmill the dude. Somebody threw a bottle at both of them. But it was me who ducked. This was before cell phones, okay? They shoved past me, fighting right out the door. I ran after them. The dude got Graham in a sleeper hold. Somebody came out and tried to break them up and got a boot to the stomach.

I remember that parking lot, Cheri says. All those cars turned off. One streetlight. This was summer, probably. Finger Shapes had his arm crooked around Graham's neck, and he was kind of butting his head into Graham's. Graham was pure scream. I mean, Cheri says, you know those bugs that hang out under a streetlight? Flecks and swarmy? Graham was screaming so loud I think he spooked them all away. Then I saw Finger Shapes go mursh, like the word mursh, very clear, and he fell away from Graham, hit the asphalt. He had his hands cupped under his mouth, and he was kind of swaying. It looked like he was catching his face, like his face was pouring into his hands. Graham spat. He was still screaming. Words, not words, maybe words. Some girl ran up to Finger Shapes. She stepped back. Holy shit, she said. He ate his mouth off, she said. He ate his lip. Oh my God. That guy ate his—oh my God.

You could hear the nu metal, but muffled. It was definitely summer.

Get a towel, the girl yelled. Don't let him leave.

I went up to Graham. He was kneeling. Streaks of dark liquid dribbled down his chin. I rubbed his back. Everybody from the party began to herd outside. Somebody must've called the cops. They sent one car into the parking lot and kept three or four in the street. Blue lights and flashlights. The music got turned down. Cops hauled me off to one side. They handcuffed Graham. One cop had a baggie. He asked about details. I'm not sure I got the order right, because I kept staring at that baggie. There was a lip in there. Bottom lip. Half a smile. Maybe a little bit of a tongue.

"What did it look like?" I ask. We're slower than all the other cars. "What did the lip look like?"

Cheri shakes her head.

Marianne's awake. Her sleeves are pulled up. "It's not right," she says.

"Yeah," Cheri says. "They just handcuffed him with all those fuckers—" She shakes her head again.

"No," Marianne says. "I mean, that's not what happened."

Somebody honks at us.

"You weren't even there," Cheri says to Marianne.

"Wait," I say. "What did the lip look like?"

"But Graham told me it was a different girl," Marianne says. "He said it was Bethany. Except they weren't going out then. She was just some girl. But she was there, and her boyfriend was there. And Graham tried to make out with her. And he bit her boyfriend. Nobody was making finger shapes."

"You want to hear the fucked up shit?" Cheri says, ignoring Marianne. "They made *T-shirts*. Those fuckers at the party made *T-shirts*. CANNIBAL GRAHAM. With an X through Graham's face. They spread a bunch of shit about how he tried to eat the dude. They called the paper and talked all this shit about Graham. About Jacqui. The villa."

"Cheri, you weren't there," Marianne says. "None of his friends were even there."

"He went to jail," Cheri says, still looking at me. "Nine months. Mayhem."

Somebody passes us on the shoulder of the freeway, honking the whole time. Cheri honks back, honks again.

"Stop it," I say.

"You're gonna kill us," Marianne says.

But Cheri keeps honking.

℘

Oakland surprises you with wildflowers. Potholes and adobe make sense. Shrivel-faced ladies muttering and tying a blanket to their shopping cart. Art deco and rickety Victorians, gangs of scowls in ski jackets, old Korean men smoking in recliners in the middle of the sidewalk, the watery reek of sunburnt butterscotch and pigeon whiz, tank-tops and yelling, bicycles and blight. But also yellow wildflowers, purple myrtle trees. Jasmine. Hedgerows and pastel houses. Swamp coolers and milk crates. Power lines a little higher than the roofs and a wideness everywhere the color of bleached slate.

We cruise Shattuck. Marianne is playing with the radio. "He moved to San Francisco after he got out of jail," Marianne says. "He ran away for a while."

We get to their driveway, pull in and idle. Cheri puts her elbows on the steering wheel. Marianne gets out of the car. I watch her peek in the mailbox.

"He was doing the soundboard for my friend's band, and they slept together," Cheri says. "Him and Marianne."

Marianne drifts up the stairs, turns the key.

Twice a year. I only see her twice a year.

"Jacqui doesn't talk to any of us anymore," Cheri says. "He just does his grin. Big Graham can't even remember who's who. The dogs remember me. They like me. Every year Jacqui throws Graham a birthday party. Maybe even threw him a party when he was in jail. When he ran away.

I didn't go to those." She stares out the window at her house. "He met Marianne right here. This house. Technically, he was going out with Beth then. You know what I mean?"

I think on that. "Can you tell me what the lip looked like?"

"We all love him," Cheri says. "Do you know anybody like that? You really love them? And a lot of other people love them too? And you can talk to those people and they know what you're talking about. They know because you all love them, that person." I look and see that she's pressing the gas pedal, even though the car is off.

"Sorry," she says. "Nevermind."

She gets out and goes into the house. I follow her. Marianne is sitting on the couch. She has her Mickey Mouse sweater pulled over her knees. Cheri goes into her bedroom and I sit down with Marianne.

"He told you about all that shit?"

Marianne shrugs. "Sure."

"You guys stopped seeing each other."

She shakes her head. "Not over that. I don't like his friends either." She sneezes and wipes her nose. "They're too nice. Everybody's too nice. He's too nice."

"And that's weird?"

"I don't know if I'd call it weird." She stares at the wall. "Are you going to ask me anything? Please don't ask me anything."

We sit for a while, not talking. Cheri comes out of her room in just a towel. "Does anybody need to use the bathroom?"

We say nothing. She goes into the bathroom.

"I'll get your mattress," Marianne says. She leaves for her room. There was a joke I made when we first hung out about taking the BART to Germany. And Marianne said please, let's go. It was cold that night, windy, that sharp and creepy Bay Area cold. We were walking by the piers. Germany I meant to be a joke, kind of. But I don't know what Marianne thought. We've never mentioned that joke again.

Marianne drags the mattress from her room, tosses it on the floor. I lie on my stomach and close my eyes. I hear Marianne kneel beside me. She touches my back. I turn over and look up at her. "Was his dick big?" I ask.

Marianne squints at me and smiles a little. "Why do you act like we can talk like that? We can't talk like that."

We listen to Cheri in the bathroom. She gets out of the shower. Turns the sink on. Whistles in long, high notes.

"I had this boyfriend in high school," Marianne says. "He said he didn't want to have sex. He just wanted to see what I looked like when I wasn't awake."

"Oh."

"Is that creepy?"

"Are you asking me?"

"I think so."

I stare at Marianne's face. I think of her lip, ripped off, how much a bottom lip might wriggle in your mouth, pink and chewy, a seagull intestine. Or maybe not. Maybe dry, like a pork rind. Someone else's lip in your teeth. Jacqui and Big Graham brushing each others' teeth. Jacqui squeezing toothpaste from his huge tube, and Big Graham opening wide. Then Jacqui rocking the bristles back and forth, easing into the molars, asking Big Graham what he feels. Just them in that enormous villa. Graham in Oakland, sobbing into Marianne's neck. Cheri in the next room, still awake. Jacqui's boyfriends in the water tower. Iron fountain in the courtyard, dry. All of the wine country's light, which is only decent if you go outside.

"Are you scared of me?" says Marianne.

It's day now, way too bright to even dream of sleep.

LOOK! LOOK! FEATHERS

Snow You Know and Snow You Don't

Some of it's a secret, but mostly it's embarrassing. Like how squishy my head gets. Over the facts and snow of this place, which are both weird. Snow falls into hazards, looks chewed and combed. People crash north of Redding and south of Dunsmuir. They wear North Face and skid around, confused. Snow is something they're new about. Like the orange-robed monks, like the aliens under the mountain. They think we're all loggers and wives, sluice pans and burl. When they see someone with a flannel jacket and an ankh tattoo on their forehead, they're like, huh?

They don't know shit, especially about the roads. How you can bicycle between Shasta City and Weed, the only stretch of I-5 you can legally bicycle, which is almost like a deal with the snow. What about this, the snow says. I'll fall so much the passes close, okay? Then when it's April and sunny, when the juniper berries shine like pellets of clear soda and the wasps are out scanning for burnt cedars and I'm all sooty and ugly on the medians, then you can ride your bicycle right on the freeway, go ahead. But don't worry. You don't have to listen to the snow. Not yet.

Another thing I may not show you right away is the lady in the bathtub. She lives in the Pollard Flat Station diner. Dan Mac and I go there still, even though I feel guilty to eat all those fried eggs with you inside. He calls and I throw the pillow at the phone. He picks me up in his taxi van at seven, just off his night run, and we drive to Pollard Flat for breakfast. He drinks from a thermos of Kool-Aid with caffeine pills crushed inside. His mustache is blue-ish. I lay his jacket over my knees and yawn into my fist, rub my belly a little, and wonder if you're awake too. Morning wipes the mountain of haze and Dan Mac goes, "Yep, still big. Still got us."

But the lady in the Pollard Flat bathroom, the lady is a mannequin. She's got a black cotton dress, high-collared, like a Victorian schoolteacher. She's missing one hand. The other's got a plunger. Her face is endlessly-okay-with-things, not shocked how some dolls look. But if you touch her, she screams. The speaker's in the showerhead. It's a black tooth kind of joke. It's a syrup on your bacon thing. Hell, you may never think it's funny. I don't, but I get it. Your mother's name is Eureka, she's never been east of Reno, she's the only girl bartender at the VFW because she's the only one quiet enough to snatch the guys' car keys, and she gets it.

Dan Mac is somebody with a funny sense of things. He'll let me order buttermilk stacks and an extra side of sausages, but then he insists on reaching over and cutting them up. He says it's good to go easy on my tubing. Then I don't feel like eating anything. But maybe it's me. Maybe you'll hit it right off.

Last January, when we first found out about you, I felt—well, I felt along the weather. Some of the worst snow in years. You couldn't see the mountain for weeks and it was cold enough to make your knuckles blush. The drifts got so high that nobody left their apartments, or needed a ride, not even to the casino in Yreka. So Dan Mac just drove around, didn't even light up his sign. He played Snake on a cell phone and parked every now and then to scrape ice off his windshield. We weren't sure about rent. Dumped the sock of laundry quarters. Our landlord lived down the street. "You up to it?" Dan Mac said. "I'm not the egg," I said. He made me wear two pairs of gloves. He needed me along. We walked. Dan Mac slaughtered the door with his fist. It opened. The landlord still had his robe on, a ponytail. Dan Mac stood there like a hump of instant potatoes.

"Just a minute," the landlord said. He smelled like marijuana. The door closed.

Dan Mac looked at me. I remembered I wasn't wearing makeup, and I was glad.

The landlord came back with glasses on and a little receipt book.

Dan Mac took out the money envelope and started counting.

The landlord cocked his head at me. "You okay?" he asked. "Little sick?"

I shook my head, stared at his eyebrows.

"Vitamin D," he said. "It's what you get from the sun. This weather, our immunities ain't up to it."

Dan Mac dropped the envelope. All the money spilled across the front step. "Fuck," Dan Mac whispered. He reached to pick the money up but sat instead, Indian-style, to count. The landlord put his hand on the doorframe. I pivoted a little and squeezed my arm and imagined I was just another tenant, waiting in line to pay, patient and uninvolved. Nausea swam up and left in a little burp. The landlord shook his head, sighed. Dan Mac took a bill off the landlord's shoe and snapped it crisp. Drifts blew around us, and pretty soon the landlord put his receipts back in the pocket of his robe.

In our living room, Dan Mac tried to light a match against the TV.

"It's glass," I said. "That's not how it works."

I was sitting on the couch, trying to keep my posture, sipping one of those citrus drugs. You drop it like Alka-Seltzer and it's got a whole anthem of vitamins.

Dan Mac dropped the match and smooshed it into the carpet with his shoe. "Fucking Doctor Landlord McHealthy Shits."

I found a lighter and threw it to him.

He lit up and I was worried he'd catch his mustache on fire, waving the cigarette around like that. "Used to be a person handles his own business," he said. "Listens, okay, nods maybe. Like sympathetic. Not do this, do that. Feeling stuff is good. Tough stuff, buddy stuff. You know, I've had a horse in that cart or some shit."

"It's not a sin to give people advice."

"Did I say 'oh please'? Did I say to go bless us with his big head?"

"Vitamins. It's just vitamins."

Dan Mac blew a ring and grunted.

"That's how he is with everybody," I said. "You know that. He's like a big dad or something."

Dan Mac walked over to a corner, crouched on his haunches. His back was to me and I could see the smoke snaking up, like from his hair.

"Don't do that," I said finally. "You're making me— I can't see if you're burning off your whole face or what."

He stood and turned to me. He put the cigarette out on the knee of his jeans but held onto the stub and walked over and knelt before me where I was sitting on the couch not drinking that God-awful vitamin soda but holding the glass, which was shaking a little because of my hands.

Dan Mac held up the stub. "This," he said, "is it. Boom."

"Okay," I said.

He made claw fists with his hands. "You can't fucking believe how much I love you," he said. "Can you? You can't, right?"

I put the glass to my forehead but it wasn't cold anymore.

Dan Mac laid his hand on my thigh, cigarette stub between his fingers still.

"Can you please not touch me with that?" I said.

He moved his hand.

"No, that," I said, pointing to the stub.

Dan Mac looked at it. Then he stood and closed his eyes. He opened his mouth and put the cigarette stub in his mouth, chewed it and gagged right away. He spit the thing out and started to hock, looging up grains and wet scrap. And I knew what he meant and I did love him for it, even though he would smoke a whole pack that night in the kitchen with the blinds drawn and the toaster going, a loaf of toast, but I was scared because it wasn't the kind of love you're meant to handle. There's watch-this love, and then there's see?-see? love. Hell, any of it. It all makes you too tired for talk. Instead I had to do something like hand him that glass of stupid citrus bullshit, which I did. He drank a gulp and sprayed it right back out, and then he drank the rest down okay.

Maybe you'll want dreadlocks. Maybe you'll be in the newspaper for basketball. You might learn to snowboard or like hot dogs. You'll never trust the other girls, though you'll want to so bad, especially the pretty ones, especially your friends. Boys'll tease you but their voices will break. If you want to play the clarinet, we'll get you one. Might be from the pawnshop. We'll need to talk about the money stuff, what people call "situations," but I'll make Dan Mac lay that out. Nothing's fair. Your fingers'll callus, even when you're reading about red nails in the magazines. But listen, they make recorders out of cedar at a place in Dunsmuir. I think so anyway. I don't understand trees. There's a lot I won't know, or won't fess up because I'll be embarrassed. You'll cut such thin-lipped looks at me, no mercy. If I seem dumb, it's only because I'm trying so hard to be sure. But I'll hurt you. God knows it. I'll say something about your body, even though I know better, and you'll lock yourself in the bathroom, and it's just because I want to be your best friend, but I already told you about those. Maybe you'll go for Hello Kitty or halter tops, and Dan Mac will punch a light bulb or something. We'll laugh at him a lot, I hope. We'll let him run ahead of us and snort like a giraffe and pick us dandelions and spill popsicles off their sticks and we'll share a look like gee whiz, but we'll never say gee whiz because only Dan Mac would say something retarded like that. And first you won't tell me about the boy. Then you will. I'll say something and you'll say "Mom!" but you'll be thinking on what I said, I know. Don't worry. I know. I'll wash the pillowcases, keep a darning needle in my teeth. I'll want to ask you what happened but I'll bite my lip. I'll put extra cheese on things and when it's just the two of us, I will say I'm sorry, I'm sorry. You'll make me cry. You'll make me sit in my nightgown when everybody else is asleep and put my sunglasses on, I'll be crying so much. Baby, it's fine. Girl, it's all good. Sometimes I'll talk that way. Uh huh. Roll your eyes, but I ain't about to quit. I'll try to like the same songs you do, but you'll laugh at me, and I'll smile, like I'm not hurt. One night I'll boil some water and pour it in a mug and dump a packet of Swiss Miss in that water, some allspice and a few of the little marshmallows, then Dan Mac'll walk through the kitchen and put a few of the big marshmallows in that water, and we'll drink our hot chocolate and maybe it's snowing, and you'll say, "This is really good, Mom. How do you make it? Show me how." And I'll say, "You know you're the sweetest and smartest girl on Earth." And I'll unbraid your hair and brush your hair and it will be the longest, prettiest hair, stupidly long, and some of your hair will smell like pomegranates and some like charcoal and all of that hair will fall all over the kitchen floor and run the floor like some of these cold streams that can't seem to get away from the mountain fast enough, but I will make you promises and keep those things. I'll quake with keeping. And all of your hair will end up right here in my hands.

c/っ

Dan Mac drives people home. "Bill's good people," he says. Or he talks about Ashleigh and her kids, Rosenberg and his Powerball tickets. He knows them all. One time an old man got out of jail in Yreka. He'd been there a while. Twenty-five years or so, nobody to wrangle bail or holler. The other inmates liked him. He was quiet. They called him Mister. Story goes he was working at the mill in Weed and one day the foreman started pointing at him, yelling something, and this Mister grabbed the foreman's hand and ran it under a circle saw. Twenty-five years, but mostly just to keep him somewhere. He didn't seem to mind. So then he's finally out. Now what? He calls a cab. Dan Mac shows up. Mister asks for the marina by Shasta Lake. Dan Mac tries to make small talk and the guy's nice enough, but one word, two words. So Dan Mac drops him off but doesn't drive away. He watches the guy walk up the road from the marina toward the bridge. The guy climbs the guardrail. Then Dan Mac starts honking his horn like crazy, and Mister's so jittered he trips back onto the road and breaks his hip. Dan Mac speeds him to the hospital and it's a big story, everybody wants to attaboy Dan Mac and clink his glass—but Dan Mac chews the attention like cud, calls the paper himself to ask if they want another interview, until we're all a little weirded out.

Sometimes, in bed, he tells me the story again, always ending it like "I just cared. Everybody was wanting me to shut up just because I cared. I don't get it. Just tell me, Eureka. You tell me why." And the thing is, I'm not supposed to tell him why. What I'm supposed to say is "People" and shrug and take my shirt off and rub his shoulders. There's how-about-that love. There's tell-me-I'm-not-crazy love. People flail in the muck of their need, and there's a love like cleaning up after.

We met on the phone. I knew who he was, kind of—the crazy cab driver. But one night this dude at the VFW needed a ride. One of the soldiers—Mitch, young, yokel, stint of Iraq in '03 and slipped into the fire academy with his very first round of college money—likes to bring his forest fire buddies around. They tip like city boys. The other soldier folk don't like them. Something about M-16s versus hoses, I guess. These young firefighters clang their bottles, pick nu metal on the jukebox, try to play beer pong on the pool tables. Well, one day this old dude, Gene— 'Nam, corduroy suit—swore and got up and told everybody "Mitchell is only technically allowed one guest, right?" But nobody said anything. He sat. There was no fight. The firefighters clustered at a table and yelled jokes about guests of Gene's ass, mocked poor Gene as he got drunker and drunker. Usually he's a three-beer guy, but he wouldn't leave. Soon it was only them and him. And Gene sat there making patterns of stains with his bottles, trembling. What could I do? Gene was right about the rules, but I needed the money. And besides, what could Eureka the girl bartender really do?

"I'm sorry," I whispered to Gene.

He shook his head. "There's no such thing as that."

So I called up the cab company and Dan Mac answered. For some reason, he was doing dispatch himself that night. When I told him the address, he snorted. "Plastered on the Patriot Act," he said.

He sounded like an asshole. "No," I said. "Just this sweet old guy."

When he got there, he was twirling his car keys around his finger. "Taxi!" he yelled.

Gene got up from the bar and went over to the coat rack to put on a pair of galoshes.

Dan Mac walked over to the table of firefighters. "You boys call a cab?"

One of the dudes jerked his head toward me. "Mommy called one for Grampsy Fagfoot over there."

When Dan Mac noticed Gene in the corner, he started shaking his head. "Dude," he said. "You know who that guy is?"

The firefighter was drunk. He staggered out of his seat, and Mitch tried to grab his elbow, but the firefighter shook him off. "Why should I give a shit who that guy is?"

Dan Mac bit one of his keys. "Gene over there, flew a fucking helicopter through a rice paddy, okay? The Vietcong had this paddy fucking surrounded. Mortars, rockets. They had three American guys captured, and they were putting rifles in their backs and making them take their clothes off. They shot 'em. All three. Then they hear this big whir, and there's a fucking helicopter flying at them ground-level through the jungle. Gene fucking flew that helicopter through their chink fucking faces. The whole paddy of them. Cut 'em down like pins."

Gene looked at me. I frowned, trying to read him. He shrugged with his lip.

"Bullshit," the firefighter said. "You can't fly a helicopter through trees."

Dan Mac hollered Gene's name. He walked over. There were seven firefighters, including Mitch, who was scrutinizing his beer bottle like he was gluing a bee together. They were all woozy. The guy talking to Dan Mac crossed his arms and stumbled over his chair a little.

"These kids," Dan Mac said, "want to tell you that you didn't watch three of your friends get shot in the back."

Gene didn't say anything. I couldn't see his face.

The firefighter held up his hands. "That's not it."

The Miller sign on the back wall pulsed. It cast a weird green over the photographs of pickaxes and men posing with bear heads. The whole bar isn't much bigger than a cabin. There's an American flag tacked under the big fluorescent overhead so things don't get too bright.

"Mac," Gene said. He sighed. "You can't fly a helicopter through trees."

Everybody started to laugh. Gene, Dan Mac, the firefighters. Fat belly hee-haws, with lots of cussing and oh-man and single claps and exaggerated tear wiping. "Crazy fucking Dan Mac!" Mitch yelled.

You'll never understand men. It's not that they're so weird, it's just they leave you going "Really? Are you kidding? That's it?" But something about Dan Mac standing there hamming it up with the firefighters and looking so light on his feet and easy in his skin made me wipe the shot glasses faster and slower.

A few whiskey rounds later, courtesy of the firefighters, Gene and Dan Mac left. I ran after them. "Hey," I called. Dan Mac turned. I smiled. "That was pretty stupid."

He gave me a sort of lemon grin and began to walk away.

"I mean," I said. "Are you okay to drive?"

Dan Mac squinted and laughed. He scooped a chunk of snow and tossed it at me, gently. I caught it. We stared at each other. Gene yelled, "Jesus Christ, I'm freezing."

Pretty soon Dan Mac was picking me up at the grocery store, the laundromat. We started driving to the Hungry Moose. We'd eat meat loaf and drink dishwater coffee. We talked about growing up around here, rock quarries and bison burgers. He told me the reason he was doing dispatch himself that night was he used to live with the dispatcher lady and now he didn't. I told him how I was born near Beale Air Force Base, but my father left us to keep on in the Air Force. Dan Mac didn't interrupt or try to patch my head up. He's a cab driver. He knows better. Later, sitting in parkas on lawn chairs and drinking wine on the balcony of his apartment, I told him about my mother—how she'd died, how young I still felt, how the cold made me more than cold, how I never did intend to acclimate, how I dream of cornstalks and watch buses—and he didn't make any jokes. He smoked, but he held me pretty well.

Wow, we sound like a couple of winners. Let me tell you something silly. You'll never want to hear about this, so I'm telling you. One night, three a.m., we lay on the carpet all covered in breath. We were high and lazy as honey. Dan Mac cussed like he could afford it. Then he got this piece of strawberry shortcake out of the refrigerator. He dumped the shortcake onto my stomach and moved a strawberry up and down my body, over my breasts, my neck. I laughed and I was really embarrassed. But Dan wasn't doing it to be romantic. He licked strawberry juice off his fingers and kissed me. He was just silly. I loved him a lot then. There's a freeze-frame kind of love. It's a love that begs. Stay right there, it says. You close your eyes and try to keep the box of tissues and the couch and the beanbag chair in their exact poses. I couldn't keep loving him that way, but I remember that night, which should count for something.

☙

"At the VFW," I said. "I'm a bartender."

The doctor looked up from his clipboard. "You drink?"

"Never." My back felt cold. Everybody bitches about those green things they make you wear, but I want to bitch about them too. I'd put off this visit for a good long while.

"They smoke in there?" the doctor asked.

"It's allowed, yeah."

The doctor shook his head and wrote more. "You shouldn't be working at all, especially not there."

"I mean, I take breaks."

"Have you experienced any vomiting, bleeding, spotting?"

"At the bar?"

"All over."

"My stomach's been acting up a lot, yeah. I try to eat saltine crackers."

"NVP is actually an indicator of a healthy first trimester. So that's good. Bad as it feels."

That stuck in my head. Bad as it feels. Feels as it bads. It feels as bad. As bad feels it.

We talked some more. He prescribed prenatal vitamins. Suggested rest. Always with the rest. Other people collected my blood and urine, but they didn't run the ultrasound. Not yet, they said. Okay, I said, because they should know, right?

In the waiting room, Dan Mac helped me put my coat on. "I've got a surprise," he said.

Ever since the thing with the landlord, Dan Mac was trying and trying. He bought airplane pillows for every chair in the house. It was wearing me out. "Okay," I said.

We drove south from the doctor's office in Yreka. It was cold but clear. Fields north of the mountain looked like the moon. Shasta's a volcano, after all, which everybody forgets. We drove past Weed, the mountain getting bigger. We hit the woods, junipers and oaks, then pulled into Shasta City, past hitchhikers in tie-dye and hitchhikers in flannel. Past the Days Inn where the truckers park, their semis single-file along the shoulder like stabled horses. Through downtown, the co-op next to the church cafe, the gun store next to the bookstore. Past the VFW. Sometimes Dan Mac turned onto one street then turned back, like he was unsure or he was really milking the drive. I didn't know which.

All the way to the on-ramp, where he saw the van. We pulled up and parked alongside. Dan Mac took my hand and we walked to the van.

Two people, a man with a gray beard down to his chest and a black girl with cornrows. They had a table set up. A sign: $$ OR WHAT U CAN. They were selling T-shirts with dragons and Bible quotes. Honey in old mayonnaise jars. Hemp jewelry. And in the middle of the table was a glass thing, about the size of a computer monitor, but clear, like a giant ice cube. Inside were these huge mosquitoes, petrified. Except their wings moved. Just a twinge.

"Everything must go," the man said. He had a weird voice, like telling a joke he didn't much like.

"You guys still have those necklaces?" Dan Mac asked.

The girl picked up a hemp necklace. Lots of beads and some kind of black stone for a pendant.

"Tell her what it does," Dan Mac said. He raised his eyebrows at me like, this'll be good.

"Hemp does what hemp does," the man said. "The beads I can't talk about. That stone we found near Tulelake, in a creek bed behind the pillow factory."

"What?" Dan said, annoyed. "That's not the right one."

The man looked at the girl. She shrugged. "Fuckin' A."

"Wait," the man said. "You mean the bird necklace?"

Dan Mac winked at me. "Yep," he whispered.

The man fished around in his pockets. He pulled out another necklace. This one hemp too, but there was no pendant and instead of beads were all these tiny bones. "Bluebird bones," the man said. "Happiness, safe journeys. All that stuff."

"How much?" Dan Mac said.

"Are those real?" I said, pointing to the mosquitoes.

"They're blessed," the girl said. She picked up the cube and shook it. Nothing happened. Then the mosquitoes began to move, slowly, contorted. Graybeard put his hand on the girl's head. "They're not for sale," he said.

"Wait," I said, still watching. "That's not—"

"Just the necklace," Dan Mac said. He was smiling too big.

"We take cash and Visa," Graybeard said. He paused. "In this realm, I mean."

Dan Mac handed him a twenty. Graybeard gave him the necklace, found a piece of paper and wrote something, then took a Polaroid camera from under the table and snapped a photo of the paper. He handed the photo to Dan. "Your receipt," he said.

Dan Mac clasped the necklace around my neck. We hugged and I kissed his cheek. "We're in it," he whispered, and I squeezed him. But listen—I want to tell you something. The whole time we hugged, I was watching the girl. She didn't touch the cube, and the mosquitoes kept getting slower and slower. Touch the fucking cube, I wanted to scream. But she just fiddled with her hair.

On the car ride back, I threw up. Dan Mac gave me water out of the emergency jug. He hugged me and I said, "I'm sorry," and he tore the necklace off me and threw it out the window. My neck burned. "It's not your fault," he said, trying to hold my hand. "It's all me. Fuck." I moved my hand away because I'd just wiped my mouth and I felt gross. "Watch the road," I said, coughing. He slowed down, and held the steering wheel tight as shit.

At home, Dan made me some soup. He cut up fresh garlic. He put me under all these blankets on the couch, and then he sat cross-legged at the foot of the couch and watched me while I ate..

"Have some yourself," I said, sipping the soup.

"I'm fine," he said.

"Listen, would you leave me alone?" I said. "Please, would you just turn around even."

He kept sitting there. Dan Mac's apartment has this big world map on the wall, DVDs and spoons all over the floor. One window has a garbage bag for a curtain. My love is a please love. I'm not saying it's love at all. That's what scares me. Dan Mac stood. He walked into the kitchen. When he came back, he had his coat on. "You need to grow up," he said.

"Dan—" I said.

"You want me to turn around, then you want to see my face, then what?"

I pulled the blankets near my mouth. "Would you—" I said.

"You don't even know what you want *yourself* to do," he said. "Your own fucking body. Did the doctor say that? I bet he did. I'm Eureka!" he yelled. He danced around. "Look at me, I'm Eureka! Aww, come on mister, give me your keys."

I scrunched my body. I wanted to cry but couldn't.

Dan Mac screamed and grabbed his hair. Then he put his hands over his face. He stumbled into the kitchen and came back with a glass of water, which he held out to me. I took it and he took the soup bowl. He walked away from me and set the soup bowl on the floor, staring at it. "It's so big," he said. "It's so big, what I feel. And you treat it like it's a marble or something. I don't know how you do that."

"I don't mean to," I said.

He looked at me. Then he said, "Are you still sick?"

"I'll be fine. The doctor said NVP is good."

"What's that?"

"Morning sickness."

"Okay," he said. He held up his hands. "He's a doctor."

"You should drive," I said. "You'll be late."

He walked over and crouched by me. He took my face in his hands. "You know what I want to do is just stay here with you. Right?"

I kissed his forehead. "I know," I said.

He held my face against his forehead. I could taste his skin, feel his eyebrows twitching under my chin. There's never enough yes-love. They ask you is-this-right, is-this-the-right-spot, and there is only that heavy way you try and the shudders and sounds, but there's a part of you that has enough love and a part of you that doesn't, and the yes always seems to open you up and show the wrong one.

"Go," I said, moving my face.

He rubbed his eye. "Okay."

When he left I felt sick. I tried to eat more soup and threw up. Sucked an ice cube and threw up. Took a nap and felt better. I wasn't sure of the time when I woke up, but the TV was playing infomercials and I closed the bedroom window because of the wind. I went into the bathroom and shaved one leg, dry, then put the razor back. I looked at myself in the mirror, touched my pimples. Bloated my face like a whale and made fish lips. Turned on the shower and flipped the plug so the bathtub would fill. I took off all my clothes. I walked out into the bedroom while the water warmed. It felt funny to walk around naked. Like not embarrassing. I went into the kitchen and ate some peanut butter with my fingers and put my butt in the refrigerator and laughed and yawned. Dan Mac was out, sign lit, taking care of good people. That's what I felt. I'm trying to tell you exactly what I felt, which is easier when you like what you feel.

I climbed into the bathtub. I left the shower running too. It felt good. My back tingled. Maybe I fell asleep. A star opened in my head and filled me. Am I in the snow now? The shower walls are white, but yellow too, from tar residue and steam, tobacco and hot water. Water going down me. My toes hurt. I'm shivering. Something is happening. When I feel more, I reach down. There are streaks on my fingers. Applesauce. Indicator. Bad as it feels. Thing. Life thing. Is this brown? Chocolate's brown, mud is, and gold. What color is this? I don't know. I'm dumb on colors. Trees. I don't call it anything. It's blood and thing. I don't call it anyone. "Oh," I say. "Lord."

I wipe it on the walls. Lines of it. Now it's blood. There's a lot of blood. And pain. Should I call somebody? Who's in charge of all this blood? Where is the face?

The shower runs, rust on the knobs, steam swamping up the bathroom. Water is going down me. Water around here, from Shasta Lake, barges of winter ice. All that water and blood. Water, how you can't let it freeze the pipes. Water with its traces of tin. "Chlorine and deer guts," I say, looking at the streaks, wiping them on the wall, wiping and wiping. "Juniper berries. Sleet. Gas. Run-off. Silt, shit, skin, skin, skin—" Like mostly skin, I thought, like I was stuck, wiping and wiping, like I couldn't imagine there was anything beneath a skin at all, and I'm crying now and wiping, even though I know I'm wrong, all that water is wrong, there's no skin, there's all the rest of everything right there to touch and how I have to touch it even though it's nothing at all now except it is because I'm touching it and I'm touching something, I know I am, you're mine, yes, your touch can't be wrong, it's yours, it's how you feel everything, whether it's real or it's yours or you're wiping it or it won't come off or it keeps smudging under all of the water and you keep wiping and where did all that water come from and who said it could? Not me. The bathtub is full of blood and me.

∽

Dan Mac takes a piss. I hear him come in. He takes a piss and turns off the bathroom light, climbs into bed. It's a little after dawn. He puts his arm around me and strokes my back.

∽

This is when we start to go to Pollard Flat. That diner. What I do is start putting pillow stuffing under my shirts. Clumps of paper towel, too, sticking it all to me with duct tape. I eat butternut squash and lima beans, barley lentil soup and V-8. Burgers and lasagna and I bloat. One night, Dan Mac brings me a bowl of ice cream with a pickle, and we laugh, because it is funny. People ask about you at the bar, and I clutch my back and give them a keep-on-keeping-on kind of look. They tip big. "She's gonna be so damn cute," they say. We don't visit the doctor. Who asked them.

Dan Mac's acting like it's temporary. He's keeping me in good shape. The tubing, he says. Why we keep on, I don't know. You can't hear me anymore, I guess. Most of the people in this world would call us weird, or some would say we're just not giving up. But they're wrong. When people say "I give up," they mean "Show me what's next." What we're doing is true giving up. Giving ourselves up to all the quiet and sternness above us, the mountain and its weather. Still big, still got us. Dan Mac tells me to keep covered, doesn't let himself see me naked. He falls asleep in the kitchen. I don't know what we're doing, but I feel like we're trying to float.

Yeah, Dan Mac knows. One night at the VFW, it was just me and Gene. Bad snow, especially for March. Disco on the jukebox. Gene got up and fed the jukebox some quarters and swore when the song didn't change.

Then this guy walked in. He was white. I mean wrapped in it. White ski cap, white sunglasses, white gloves, and white bandages all around his face except his lips, which were pale. He had a long gray trench coat that covered him down to his boots. He sat at a stool and put a military ID on the bar. "Private," he said.

Gene walked back up to the bar. He looked at the guy for a while then he glared at me. Don't ask, he mouthed.

But the guy saw. He laughed. "It's not like that," he said. He asked for a vodka cran. "I'm just allergic to the sun," he said. "I was over in Kabul, and I got really sick. They ran some tests, and I guess a person can just get allergic to the sun." He shrugged.

Gene nodded and blew into his hands like he was cold. Nodded again. "Yes, sir," he said. "God bless you."

After his three beers, Gene left, and then it was only me and Private. We talked. Sure we did. I wasn't going to stand there with the guy like something holy was happening. He told me he was just passing through, driving back up to his family in Medford. I told him about the bicycles on I-5, the sausages at the Pollard Flat diner. He stayed until closing time.

Never took his coat off. Around three, I looked outside. The snow was pretty bad. I locked the door, turned off the sign. Then I went behind the bar, to all the switches, and I flipped them all off, including the big fluorescent under the American flag.

I couldn't see my hand in front of my face. Private's head—his bandages and cap—seemed to glow, or maybe it was just their being white.

I opened the cash register. There was a lighter in the hundreds drawer. I gave it to Private.

He held the lighter. "Never have," he said. He reached across the bar and took my hand and kissed it. I pulled my hand away. "I'm not looking for anything," he said. I didn't know how he could see with those sunglasses on.

Listen. It wasn't any kind of love. Some of these people, men and women both, they'll want to make you scream. You just wait and feel it out. See what you want to call it. There's lots of things to feel. Just because love's the big one doesn't mean it's all we can.

Outside, the snow was thick and total. I called Dan Mac.

"I turned my sign off," he said. "This is real heavy shit. Why the hell you still at the bar?"

"A guy passed out," I said. "I can't just leave him."

"Oh," Dan Mac said. "Well, bring him along."

Dan Mac didn't say anything when he saw Private, not passed out at all. He seems to have a lot of faith in people. Maybe it's on account of something he's never told me.

Private's motel was at the other end of town. At a stoplight, we made a turn, and the taxi van hit a skid of black ice. Dan Mac yanked the wheel. We fishtailed. He kept one hand on the wheel and slapped the other over my stomach and some tissues fell out, but he didn't notice. We slid into a ditch, a snowbank, real gentle-like, and Dan Mac revved the wheels for a while before he killed the engine.

We got out. Dan Mac got a shovel out of the back. He started shoveling.

Private stood there awkwardly. "I can help," he said.

So Dan Mac stopped, shrugged, and handed him the shovel. "There's just the one," he said.

I trudged out into the road. Dan Mac followed me.

"You'll catch pneumonia," he said. He took my arm. I flinched.

His breath made steam in the cold. He turned and looked at Private, who was wiping snow off the headlights.

"No," I said. "It's me."

Dan Mac looked at me. He stared. I pulled a wad of paper towels out of my shirt. Dan Mac started to tremble. "Wait," he said.

It's strange when a person rattles that hard. You start to worry he'll loosen, slough away in bits. There's an us-against-the-world love, but I was too scared to move. How can you buy into that kind of thing? When the world is the world and the us isn't. Bluebirds and volcanoes. Circle saws and pomegranates. Snow fell on the TAXI light, onto Private's white ski cap, into Dan Mac's mustache. Honeycombs of ice, and millions more around. Listen. You will always want what you can't feel. Snow is full of little things that fall, and I swear sometimes they all know each other.

LOOK! LOOK! FEATHERS

Mosquito Fog

When Russell drove the fog truck, he didn't use the siren. Lights only, an orange throb, while the smoke to kill mosquitoes gusted from a nozzle in the truck bed. Nights that Russell drove, people slept right through. But he didn't feel kind. More selfish. All that fog to himself, a cloud to drag along. He liked to drive the levee, see the fog nestle in the digger pine and sycamore. Bats careened. Fog bunched up above the Feather River, then thinned into a dark smog between the moonlight and the water. Russell didn't even mind the smell. Like honey and hand sanitizer. No one knew that Russell was the best mosquito fogger; he was too fast and good. One September, in a bout of squeamish heat, he fogged almost every night. Mosquitoes plunked in droves. Dragonflies got fat off the corpses. Russell wore a gas mask.

Before his shift, he'd some nights take his daughter to supper. Ashley was getting an AA in web design at the local JC. She had a lip stud. Russell had seen her websites. One for the local bike shop, especially. Pretty spiffy, Russell thought. Interactive trail maps. Ashley was dating the bike shop's owner, Trevor, and Russell believed himself okay with the guy, Trevor. But that September, over fajita skillets at Casa Verde, Russell learned that Ashley and Trevor were moving to Portland.

He blew on a green pepper. "You don't graduate until spring."

"It's just a thing they mail," Ashley said. "The AA. No ceremony. But anyway, we're not out until summer." She picked a lone beef strip off her plate, doused it in hot sauce.

"So," Russell said. "Am I best man material?" He tilted a grin.

"There's a huge bike race every July. Like the Olympics of bicycles.

Trevor wants to move his shop there. Do just racing stuff." She ate the beef. "You wouldn't be the best man, that's not how it works."

"Well, your mother and I got married at the clerk." He waved his fork, shrugged. "I guess you knew that."

"Officially what you do is, quote, give me away." She rubbed her neck and looked at the food. "For now it's really just the move, Dad."

"Hey, I can roll. I'm a roller."

Ashley forked all her onions to the gutter of the skillet. "Figured I would give you fair warning."

"Well, we'll email. Bet we can even video talk or something, right?"

"Right," she said. "You never go out. I mean, like bars and stuff."

"Ashley," he said. He rubbed his chin. Before their dinners he always shaved. For his fiftieth birthday, Ashley and his wife, Claire, had given him a bottle of expensive Canadian whiskey, the kind that came in a velvet pouch. Ashley was ten. She'd made a bunny out of a plastic spoon—chenille stems for ear—and tucked it inside the pouch. Once or twice a year, at otherwise insignificant suppers, Russell would grab the bottle and pretend to make the bunny drink. Ashley always laughed and asked him when he'd finally drink the stupid whiskey. Russell would wink at Claire and say, "Once in a moonbeam."

Claire had been a blackjack dealer. Though she wasn't tribally affiliated, she was popular with casino management. She could kick awake bum Keno machines. They were loosely coiled people, Russell believed, the kind of family who likes to park on the dam and eat peanut butter crackers. Once, channel surfing on a night he and Claire both had off, all three of them together in the living room—meatball subs on TV trays, yakking and joshing, Ashley high-pitched about some fresh saga—they came upon a country music video with a violin, mustached singer alone in a phone booth, surrounded by sleet and neon. At first, Russell didn't understand why the singer had such a strange face. Then he realized the man in the video was not happy, was play-acting some idea of despair, and Russell changed the channel, unnerved by the blindness of his own happiness. His luck. He felt defensive and scared, then—after mulling all this and looking for the right feeling to calm down by—blessed.

At the beginning of Ashley's senior year of high school, Claire came home from the casino complaining that the pit had been too cold. A few hours later, she collapsed in the bathroom. Russell heard. When he ran in, she was clutching her temples. Said her eyes hurt like somebody was pounding nails in. Around dawn, she died. The doctors talked about the aorta, the walls of the brain. Ashley stayed home for two months, until Russell finally stopped erasing the vice-principal's answering machine messages. Three years. That was three years ago.

Russell took a sip of Coke. He cut a black bean into halves, thirds.

"What about model airplanes?" Ashley said. "What about four wheeling? The guys at work?"

"Drive a truck all night'll make you not so into trucks," Russell said.

"That's not true."

"I'd rather have a cane than a truck."

"Dad," Ashley said quietly.

The waitress came to collect the skillets. Russell pulled a credit card from his back pocket and slid it across to Ashley. He didn't feel like talking to the waitress. Ashley took the card and asked the waitress for the check.

"Should've asked for more chips," Russell said when the waitress left. "Chip dessert."

"I'm not saying it's about you." Ashley poured hot sauce on her finger. She wiped it on the table. "I feel like, heartless. Like a bitch."

Russell winced. He leaned back in his chair. "I know it seemed—" He squeezed his forehead. Then he said "I know it seemed like we always wanted the same thing. But the thing was, we were just too tired. We had a joke. Once you moved out, we'd start fighting. That was the joke."

"You did fight. Then you'd play computer golf, and Mom would lock herself in the bathroom with her Walkman."

Russell closed his eyes. Casa Verde had a radio on, but it wasn't music. Some kind of Mexican comedy. Goofy boinging noises and exaggerated ¡Aye!¡Aye! ¡Aye!'s. "When there's a thing underneath," Russell said finally. "Things on top just sort of float away."

Ashley bit her thumb and looked at the table. "Sometimes I'll still be up and I'll get my phone out because I know you're driving. But I don't want to, like, interrupt you, so I—" She trailed off. Russell watched her face work. When the waitress came back with the credit card, Russell swiped the pen from her hand, signed the receipt, and asked her to read his name back.

"Is that an R?" the waitress said.

"That's my name, don't wear it out." He grinned. Ashley snorted and wiped her eyes a little. The waitress looked between the two of them. She left and turned up the radio.

❧

The next day, Russell installed a way to video chat. He kept his computer in the kitchen. Next to the keyboard was a coffee mug of cranberry juice. For breakfast, he'd made a pot of Kraft Dinner and peas, ate standing up, then washed the pot. The kitchen smelled like butter. There was a Cheerios box full of coupons atop the refrigerator, Claire's idea that Russell kept. A little cabinet-box of pills sat behind his computer, medicine sorted into days. Russell opened Sunday, closed the box with the mug and took the pill with cranberry juice. "Let's hear it for the stomach," he said. He wasn't much for music or talk radio, but he liked to leave the TV going in the living room, and he'd speak to whatever lights he turned on. Out the window was the fire escape, sunlight relentless, avocados squished on the sidewalk, and the churn of a riding lawnmower from the eye doctor's office across the street. Russell thought they mowed too much. After the video chat installed and asked him to reboot, he got up and opened the freezer and cracked an ice cube to suck. He emailed Ashley to let her know about the video chat. He clicked Send. He sucked ice. Waited. After an hour, he cranked his volume all the way and left the computer to watch college football on mute.

He awoke on the couch, computer bleating. When he stumbled into the kitchen and shuffled his mouse, he saw that Ashley was inviting him to chat. He clicked and they popped up, Ashley and Trevor, squinting at him from their bedroom. On the wall behind them hung a poster of guitar chords. Ashley sat at the computer, Trevor leaning over her shoulder. Both looked pretty grainy, which disappointed him.

He tried to button his shirt. "Sorry," he said. "Just got up."

"Where are you?" Ashley said.

"Eh?"

Grainy Trevor pointed at him. "Look on the lower right. There should be a box with your face in it."

"It's black. Blank, I mean."

"Yeah," Trevor said. "We can't see you."

"It's okay, Dad," Ashley said. "We can hear you. We can only talk for a minute."

"Oh."

"Got to do this tour the town thing," Trevor said. "First Sundays, round the levee and back. People look at the murals, you know. We tell 'em town stuff. Nature stuff." He had a tuft of hair below his lip. What do they call that, Russell thought. A soul patch?

"What exactly do you tell these people?" he said.

"You know," Trevor said. "Local stuff. Did you know that there are opium tunnels under the town? Right under. The Chinese, the rail workers, used to run smuggling rings."

"They got a mural of that, huh?" Russell was going to add that maybe opium fell under the guise of nature stuff, but he realized they couldn't see his grin.

"They're really fun," Ashley said. Trevor put a hand on her shoulder and squeezed. Ashley said, "All the ladies have these really terrific sun hats."

"They play frisbee golf," Trevor said.

"Frisbee golf," Russell said.

"Are you on Facebook?" Trevor asked. "They have a group on there. The Gold City Giddy-Ups."

Russell leaned back and scratched his stomach. He stuck his tongue out at the computer. He slapped the monitor. Then he said, "Well, sounds like they know how to have a good time. I'll look 'em up."

"Maybe we can come by later," Trevor said. "Try to fix your webcam."

"Ashley told me about Portland. Rains a lot up there, I hear. Lots of bums."

"You seen the lake lately, Dad?" Ashley said. "Little bit of rain might hit the spot!" She looked at Trevor and laughed.

Russell stood and turned away from the computer. "I've seen the lake."

"Really a lot of good stuff in Portland," Trevor said. He squared his shoulders. "It's not like it was, you know, a few years ago."

"Can't argue with that," Russell said. "Opportunity ain't about to stand around and wait for you to fix your doorbell. You know what they say: even Custer couldn't sleep in Little Big Horn."

Trevor laughed and crossed his arms. Ashley said, "Who says that?"

"Well," Russell said. He flourished his hand, trying to whip something up, then he noticed his hand and stopped. He sat and rested his hand on the monitor, covering the video window. The kitchen was too hot. There was a bottle of Pine Sol on the stove. Russell could name everything in the refrigerator. Bologna, corn tortillas, half-empty cans of green beans. Whenever he didn't finish a can of something, he left the can in the refrigerator, open. Across the street, they'd stopped mowing. For some reason, Russell recalled a TV show about the nature of sound. In rooms of total silence, claimed the show, with all sound engineered away, you can still hear two things: blood circulation, which makes a low thrum, and the nervous system, which makes a kind of weak mew. "I don't know," he said to the computer. "People just say things."

એડ

After Ashley and Trevor logged off, Russell joined Facebook. All the dialog boxes and prompts reminded Russell of a jogger with a cell phone, one of those no-hands jobs. He couldn't understand why young people found it fun. But what the hell, he made a profile. Left a lot blank, including Relationship Status, Birthday, Looking For—too private. For "Favorite TV Shows" he listed a few sports and added "proud fan of cal football 30+ years & strong." He uploaded an old photo of himself at the Forebay, thumb-steering an R/C boat, Claire and Ashley picnicking in the background, back from when he still smoked cigarettes. Then he searched for the group Trevor had mentioned. Gold City Giddy-Ups.

Most of them were grandparents, with pictures of cargo shorts and holiday parties. Whole photo albums named after vacation spots, shots of them looking winded near ruins, beaming next to dark-skinned tour guides and propping one foot on a ledge, wide shots with plenty of frame space for the views stressed in the captions. These Giddy-Ups had healthy lists of interests, links to their children's and grandchildren's profiles. Many seemed to take surveys ("How well do you know your garden?") or post "gifts" on each others' profiles, which so far as Russell could tell were all doodles with irrelevant labels.

Ashley was a member of the group. Clicking through her pictures— punk shows in the tire shop scrap yard, bowling with Trevor—Russell felt weird, snoop-ish, but he reminded himself that Ashley had chosen to share all this. Besides, nothing on her profile shocked him. She wasn't a secretive girl. Several of her status updates said she was tired. He clicked "Add Ashley as a Friend," then he posted a message on the main wall of the Gold City Giddy-Ups.

howdy everybody. my daughter ashley told me about this group. good to see people out and about. <g> i'm a born and bredder. class of '68. drive trucks for the rec district. still on my feet, still like a little bit of mud. kayaking and so on. my dad used to say "there's life and then there's strolling for crawdads" and i think he had a point. lookin forward to "hanging out." not sure what else to say. <g> hope everybodys friendly as they look!!! take care, russ

It didn't take the Giddy-Ups long to comment. Lots even clicked Like, which made Russell grin, until he realized that everyone on Facebook seemed to click Like all the time, a sort of enthusiasm whack-a-mole. Still, the Giddy-Ups were friendly. Men told him they were glad to see another fellow in the group, joked about being chased with cast iron pans. And all the women seemed to know Trevor and Ashley, kept complimenting Russell's photo and rattling off dates to upcoming get-togethers. Russell spent the whole day adding friends and commenting, browsing for old high school buddies, taking quizzes. By the time he looked up, it was dusk, and he'd skipped his pre-work nap.

Fogging that night he thought about how odd it was, all those retired people clicking in their dens, firing away at the computers their kids had taught them how to use, finding one face after another to stay in touch with. Even people they'd just seen. Go out for doughnuts every Thursday, drive home and post on the group wall: "Doughnuts were swell this morning, gang! Can't wait for—" and then whatever they did together. Racquetball. Bocci ball. Mostly Russell watched TV. He knew his way around the computer. He'd even post, now and then, on ESPN's college football message boards. Anonymously. And suppers with Ashley, right? Sometimes she and Trevor came over, brought brownies. He tried to remember the names of the other foggers. Winston? Wichita? He used to know, but they clocked and retired, and he'd let the names drift. There were faces, sure, all those pancake breakfasts that the Rec. District threw. Faces and vats of batter.

At the end of his shift, he idled on the levee to watch the dawn. The ridge paled into brightness. Hills like chalk being unerased. Leaves and needles braised in sun, silver blinking on the river. When he drove back into town, he passed the Bedrock Tennis Courts, saw a cluster of older folks hitting blurs of yellow fuzz, chuckling and volleying. He stopped the truck, but then he remembered he was wearing overalls. His gas mask rode shotgun. Besides, Russell thought, they figured he was the guy from the lake photo, cigarette cocked. But that photo was fifteen years old. At least.

That had been such a fun picnic. Such a fun little boat. Claire snorted when she saw him steer and chew his Marlboro. "Henry Bogart strikes again," she said. But she was smiling. She got a park ranger and made him snap a photo. Put Ashley on her lap. Told the ranger where to stand. Russell was impressed at how sharp the photo turned out. Claire must've envisioned exactly how to do it, saw just how far and how close everybody needed to be.

Russell rolled down the window and heard somebody yell "Out!" Somebody else yelled "Out my ass!" and everybody laughed. Russell left the window down and drove away.

കൗ

Two weeks later, he'd begged off every invitation from the Gold City Giddy-Ups, but he couldn't stop wasting time on Facebook. Facebooking. He'd get off his shift, check Facebook, slump to bed, blear up at noon and log on. Pretty soon, Russell had a couple private exchanges. One with a man named Orrin, who wasn't in town. He was on a permanent R/V vacation with his wife, and loved to recount minor adventures—missives, he called them. Russell told Orrin he'd been in the Air Force, which wasn't true. But Orrin didn't seem to notice: he yammed on about himself.

Another exchange was with a woman named Delilah. She worked at Foodglow, a local twenty-four hour grocery store. There wasn't much on her profile, which comforted Russell. Just a few pictures—reindeer sweater, cotton sundress—and a few favorites. Agatha Christie novels, microbrews. She had a link to a NASA live feed of the moon, which Russell found strange, but only a little. Delilah was married. Her husband's profile was private. He was not a member of the Gold City Giddy-Ups. After a few messages, Russell and Delilah began to live chat. Delilah was a fast typer, and she asked a lot of questions.

> *what does <g> mean?*
> *grin. it's pre-internet stuff. guess i'm just an old computer nerd <g>.*
> *oh ok. i just can't keep up with all this stuff! i'm still trying to figure out smiley faces.. ;-)*
> *heh, that's okay. here i'll try one: =)*
> *welcome to the 21st century lol!!*
> *oh boy! not sure if i like the sound of that, hehe.*

Delilah wanted to hear about the crawdads, then his high school tailback career. She'd grown up in a different town. All her exclamation marks buoyed his confidence. So he talked about his family, peanut butter crackers on the dam. Even hokey stuff, the ho-hums of bug fogging. Each story came easier than the last. Pretty soon the chats turned to Claire, and something about the compression of the chat box and letters that popped up quick as his fingers could pepper them, but not so quick as his mind—more patient, malleable, forgiving of revision—made him frank. He typed to hear the clack. One thing about Claire would come, then he'd admit that probably wasn't what he felt at all. He joked about Trevor and his bicycle brigade, bragged about Ashley. Delilah didn't have any kids, but she loved to hear about Ashley. So Russell talked about her website designs, told stories of her as a kid: trying to ride her tricycle into the lake;

burning her hand one Easter and calling 9-1-1 by herself; wanting a bunk bed when she was nine but being too scared to sleep on top. One night, Russell typed for a long time, letting his seat go numb, eating ramen noodles cold so he wouldn't have to interrupt himself, and he typed until he was typing about how blessed he used to feel, and how such a feeling struck him now.

like i was so busy feeling blessed and thanking my life for being itself;; that i didn't feel enough of it.... like i was keeping my life so good that i didn't know how good it was.
but it was good. that's the point.
yeah.
sorry. i wish i could say the right thing. :-(
aw, del. don't sweat it. youre doing great.
you're being so honest and amazing and i'm just an old bump on a log! i mean, i just sit around at home all day while michael's in the offfice. helps to have somebody to talk too.
pass the time. i hear that.
hey russ! pass the time! :-)
hahaha. you pass the poatoes and ill pass the time.
can i ask you something?
yes. not only yes but please do.
youre sweet. :-)
that's not a question!!
haha okay. it's about ashley.
what about her?
she's moving to portland, right?
yep.
right ....
come on! spit it out.
you keep telling me you're happy for her. but i dunno. tonight your talking

about,,,, are you really happy for her??

Russell tapped the space bar. Then held it down. The kitchen was dark, and he wasn't sure about the hour. What he knew was the chat window read *Russell is typing*, and as he held the space bar for longer and longer, he began to wonder how long Delilah would wait for his answer, if she'd grow bored and leave her computer, pat her cheeks with lotion, crawl into bed with her husband.

Then she typed something:

sorry, russ. that was a bad way to put it.

He backspaced a few of his spaces, but before he'd deleted them all she typed again:

you're a good dad. :-) <3

When he realized the <3 was a heart, Russell didn't type anything. After some time, he clicked Log Out. Then he powered off his computer. He flipped on the lights in the kitchen, the bathroom, all the bedroom lamps. Outside, he could hear crickets and drunks. He poured a glass of milk, drank one sip and dumped the rest down the sink. On the TV, most stations were garbled. But he found one playing an action movie: Harrison Ford scrunched into a ventilation duct, staring out the grate at the bad guys' boots. When Russell turned up the volume, he realized that the voices and mouths weren't in sync. He grabbed his jacket, left the house, and drove to the Rec. District garage. He used his key and climbed into the fogging truck. In the darkness, he planted his feet between the pedals. Then a sluggish glow clouded the garage, and he heard somebody clomp over and tap on his door.

It was one of the night crew, a Hmong in khaki overalls. Russell opened the door and the Hmong fluttered his eyebrows, grinning and peering. "You decent, Russ?"

"I was just about to go on shift—just trying to sort through these numbers—" he tapped the dashboard.

"You're off tonight," the Hmong said.

"I switched shifts. I'm filling in for—" he opened the glovebox, but there was only a gas mask.

"Wool? You're filling in for Wool?"

"Sure," Russell said.

"Well, the good news is that you're not due until three, but if you want an early start—" he shrugged. "Just make sure nobody's walking around, I guess. Don't want to spray any joggers or whatever."

"Joggers? This time of night?"

The Hmong laughed. "Stranger danger!" He laughed again and inspected the truck's fog nozzle, then he started shuffling back to the office. Russell felt bad not knowing his name. "Hey," he called. "You got a TV in there?"

"Wile the night away," the Hmong called.

"There's this Harrison Ford movie," Russell said. "Not bad, you know. Not one of his best."

"One verdict, over easy," the Hmong said. "Guess you better get out there and start choking some stingrays." He grabbed his throat and bulged his eyes, pretending to gag, making a joke at the other end of the garage.

❧

Russell finished before three, but he didn't feel like saying howdy back at the garage, so he drove to Foodglow. Just as he parked, something clanged into his truck. Shopping carts, a long caravan. The kid pushing them waved an apology. Then he wrestled the carts through the parking lot and slammed them into a larger row outside the entrance. The carts nested into each other, front baskets folding up, and Russell remembered how Ashley had never wanted to ride in the basket like she was supposed to, insisting always on the bottom.

Inside, he found an open tin of snickerdoodles. Right on the counter at the bakery, nobody working or watching. The cookies tasted fresh. Russell wandered in the staunch fluorescence. Jets misted toy-colored produce. Janitors dragged yellow buckets, shaggy mops. All the prepared food was swathed in plastic sheets. Hardly anyone was shopping. Those who were shopping held baskets sparsely filled: eggs, tater tots, pints of generic ice cream. Now and then someone would be standing in an aisle, holding one thing—a carton of lemonade, a can of chickpeas—staring at that thing as if it were a snow globe. There were more WET FLOOR signs than people, but Russell felt anxious, like there were shoppers he couldn't see ducking into the aisles he'd just left, wandering past the groceries he'd just touched. When had he last gone to Foodglow? Claire had never shopped there; even food needs beauty sleep, she'd say. Russell toured the whole store several times before he allowed himself a can of chili.

Then he saw Delilah at the checkout.

His first thought was to put the chili in front of his face. His mind stuttered. Did she always work this late? How was she on Facebook earlier? He hung back and watched as she bagged soap and vegetables for an old lady in a nightgown. After Delilah had bagged everything, she stooped and gave the lady a hug. She was taller than she'd seemed on Facebook. When Russell finally walked up, Delilah smiled.

"Delilah," he said.

She kept smiling.

He waved the can of chili. "Howdy."

"I'm sorry, what did you say?"

Russell looked at the beans on the label of his can. "It's Russ," he said. Even after everything he'd typed to her, especially that night, he still couldn't bring himself to finish: *Russ from the internet.*

"Did you say lilacs? Are you looking for lilacs?"

Russell set the can on the conveyer belt, and Delilah pushed the belt's stop button. "Can I help you?"

Russell was wearing overalls. His mouth felt dry and huge. "Delilah? With a D?"

"Oh!" Her face softened. "Sorry. My name's Linda."

Russell stared at the chili. He stared at the chili. He stared at the chili.

"Do you want me—" Linda said. "Maybe I can page her?"

Russell waved this off. He stared around for a minute before he spoke. "It's the computer," he said. "Playing tricks with my brain."

Linda nodded and picked up the chili. "Ring this through?"

Russell shook his head. "Hell, I don't even like that brand. Would you believe that? Here I am, and that's not even the right chili."

Sweet and gently distracted, Linda looked just like her Facebook photos. But not her photos, Russell thought. Delilah's. "You like chili?" Linda asked.

No one else was in line. Most people were too asleep to need groceries. As he stood there, Russell felt like he and this strange woman were the only people awake in the whole town, maybe the world. He felt like grabbing this lady and dunking her in blue paint, dying her the color of the website surrounding those photos. Come back, he wanted to say. I told your photos everything. Your face has to know me. The moon's in your profile. You're Delilah. Where did you go? "Chili's fine," he said. He pointed to the can Linda held. "But not that one."

৵৩

A girl sat in the fog truck. Teenaged, wearing a Foodglow apron. She sat in the passenger seat with the straps of the gas mask tied around her wrist. Her face had ripples of acne caked over by makeup, and her hair was yanked into a braid. She spun the mask by its straps. When Russell tapped on the window, she jumped, and the mask hit her in the face like an errant yo-yo.

Russell opened the door. "Don't play with that."

The girl untangled the mask from her wrist and let it clank on the floorboard. She clamped a hand over her heart and kept swallowing instead of breathing.

Russell stayed outside the cab, one foot on the rocker panel, arm balanced on the roof. He couldn't remember whether he'd locked the truck. He'd told Linda to keep the chili, and he felt gray. Flatlined. "You lost?" he asked the girl.

"I didn't think—oh my God. This would be your truck? There's a lot of trucks. Trucks!" She giggled, a splatter of wheezes.

"It sure ain't yours," Russell said.

She turned to Russell and didn't meet his eyes, pointing between him and her, a kind of eeny meeny. "Right? Oh my God. It's. You wouldn't. This was totally not—" Her eyes watered, and she shoved her knuckles in them. "I'm sorry. I have to stop. Oh God I'm stupid. I'm a fucktard." She covered her face with her apron.

Russell bounced one foot on the rocker panel. Behind his knees, he felt the ache of all his lost sleep. "First we need to calm down, okay?"

"You must think—" she sighed and tried to catch her breath. "Wow. I am so awesome at just fucking everything up. If I were good at shit, this would be like, totally different. But I saw the truck and it was like, I never see one of those trucks, right? So I thought I'd wait and see if it was you, but then I was like, wow, that's such a retarded idea. He's not gonna be like, 'Hey! Awesome! It's you!' He's gonna be like, who's this weird bitch in my truck. But then I thought what if it's not you, what if it's, like, one of your buddies, right? And I could ask them, 'Hey, where's Russ hang out?' But then I was like, oh my God, some random dude? I'm sitting in some random dude's truck? What if he, you know, does something weird? So I'm like, okay, I'll put this mask on, but it's like duh, it's a mask, it's not gonna—listen. You know me. Please. We've talked."

Russell stepped back off the rocker panel. He clasped his hands on his head. The night was warm and quiet. A Jeep banked the curb in front of Foodglow, emergency blinkers flashing, and two teenaged boys stumbled into the store holding hands. Sometimes people talked of meeting themselves in their dreams, but Russell never did that. His dreams were always him being him, not through his eyes but a little above his shoulders. Which was how he imagined this girl, slumped in her bed with a laptop. "Right," he said. He felt like he should laugh, but he couldn't.

"Do you get it?" the girl asked.

"Delilah?"

Inside her apron, Delilah seemed to melt. When she spoke again, she whispered. "There's a song. It's stupid. You haven't heard it?"

Russell shook his head.

"It's about this girl in New York," she said. "It's catchy, but it's not, like, a real name."

"Isn't it from the Bible?"

Delilah fiddled with the glovebox handle. "I guess. The song wasn't around when I was born, so maybe it's from the Bible, I don't know."

He could leave this girl in the truck. Call and quit his job. Move to some new town outside Portland, close enough to Ashley that she wouldn't worry. He'd put his computer in a garbage bag, bind the bag with twist-ties from Claire's endless stash and leave it on the curb under the avocado tree. In a few hours, the garbage man would heave the bag into a truck that never bothered Russell because he never slept decent hours. He'd lie awake. Then he'd hear the racket of the eye doctor's lawnmower, and he'd leave his bed. In the refrigerator, green beans. On the table, a gap in the dust. One less screen to worry about. More time for the other lights, which Russell knew was what he'd say to himself when he turned them all on.

"I'll drive you home," Russell said.

Delilah shook her head. "I'm on shift."

"That makes two of us." He laughed and stared at the asphalt. "You want to know something? I lied to take this shift. After you typed that thing. It's not even my shift."

"I was late," she said. "I had to leave for work, but I didn't want you to stop."

Russell climbed into the cab and shut the door. "Hand me that gas mask."

She held it out to him, and he didn't look at her, just took the mask and set it on the dashboard.

The radio squawked. "Hey rumblefish forty-five." It was the Hmong. "Loved the movie. Me and Wool both. Can't say we fall in your camp on this one. But we do need that truck back, 10-4?"

Delilah was shivering. Russell felt exhausted. Weren't they buddies? All that typing back and forth. Sure, okay, she'd turned out to be some acne-fried teenage girl, a liar in a claptrap with an old fogey, both of them wrong to sit like nothing was creepy or untoward, but didn't they trust each other? Or didn't she know how to be somebody he trusted, at least? The sane thing, he knew, was for her to snap up and scamper off, fun over, old dude sufficiently messed with. But she just sat there. Jammed with guilt, maybe. Afraid of what Russell might do, how he might punish her. But he was too tired to care about any of that. He wasn't a country singer in a phone booth. He didn't want to foist his pain on anyone. He unplugged the radio. Fastened his seatbelt. All he wanted was his friend. "You want to wear some gas masks?" he said. "Well, let's wear some."

ை

"I found this list on the internet. The loneliest people in the world. It was a joke. Like, #1 was God, and then there was, like, people who bake cookies for talk show hosts, pilots who fly cargo jets for FedEx Overnight, stupid stuff like that. It was pretty funny, though, and when you started getting into all the really depressing stuff, I thought, well, I'll send it to him. But there was this line in the beginning that made it seem—I don't know, it didn't seem as funny."

"There's websites for that?"

"Lists?"

"Well, I mean, who thinks up a list like that?"

"That's what I'm saying. The line at the beginning was like 'blah blah, just like you might suspect, most of these people involve night.' It didn't seem—you know. Helpful."

"And here we are," Russell said.

They drove the levee, fog gusting. Still an hour or so until dawn. Russell wasn't sure how much spray he had left, but he didn't care. As they drove, he pointed out where the Sierra Club had installed placards to explain about endangered flowers or rattlesnakes. Delilah clutched the gas mask. She didn't open easily, but Russell didn't prod. Just drove. Delilah talked about her mother, a nurse, practicing with her sphygmomanometer on Delilah's arm.

"That's the thing to get blood pressure," she said. "You only need the second-lowest setting, I think, to get an accurate reading. But she used to crank it all the way up. She thought it was funny." Delilah looked out the window at the river. "I never would've told you that online. Even if I was like, being the real me. I don't know how to spell sphygmomanometer, so I probably would've just kept my mouth shut."

"Seems easy to look up."

"Still."

Russell nodded.

Bats zigged from tree to tree, frenzied when they passed through open air.

"I carried Claire into the ambulance," Russell said. "I wouldn't let them put a stretcher under her. Ridiculous, me doing that. Does this look like manual labor? I didn't have the arms for it. But nobody was gonna touch her but me. And she held on. Believe me. She didn't want to let go. Only time she let go was when she had to touch her head because of the pain."

Delilah rubbed her thumb on the eyeholes of the gas mask. "My mom used to make me take quizzes for her. Pain's one tiny part of the brain trying to clue you in. And then the rest of the brain is just sort of working on whatever's messed up. So the pain is just to let you know that your body's, like, on the job."

The truck rumbled and clattered over potholes.

"How did you hack the site, anyway?"

"Linda's pictures were on my computer. I was helping her learn to use her camera—" She tapped the mask against the window. "You're the first person I really talked to from that group. I thought maybe you wouldn't catch on." She grinned shyly. "I really did love your post. I thought you sounded like—full of stories."

Russell laughed and sighed. "Full of something, all right."

Delilah turned and looked out the back of the truck. "You can't even see anything."

"Yes m'am. Dead mosquitoes."

"Is the gas, like, bad for everything? Or just mosquitoes?"

Russell pointed at the gas mask in Delilah's hands. "Let's find out."

He parked. They got out. Delilah wore her Foodglow apron and the gas mask, and Russell kept a handkerchief over his nose and mouth. They walked the levee, kicking cones the size of raccoon skulls. Catkins and acorns lay scattered, littered off the oaks. Bullfrogs somewhere close, cars not much farther. Digger pines loomed gaunt and crooked above them, branches so wispy they blurred. Below, the river was a gurgle of murk. They waded through mosquito fog. "I don't see anything," Delilah said.

"Listen," Russell said. "You're crunching 'em."

"I don't hear any crunching, either."

"Trust me."

Then Russell's lungs began to burn, and he stepped out of the fog. His chest felt fuzzy and his ears held a weird ring, but he breathed in. He couldn't help himself. He liked the smell.

"Where are they?" Delilah said. The fog was beginning to thin.

"Look for their wings," Russell said. "Sort of see-through."

Delilah got down on her stomach. She bumped the gas mask against the ground. "If they're see-through," she said, "how am I supposed to see them?"

LOOK! LOOK! FEATHERS

STAY AWHILE IF YOU CAN

We drive to breakfast in the rain. Allison has the wheel and a tissue up her nose to plug the blood.

"Stop giving me that face," I say.

She speeds through a yellow. "That's not a face."

I start to say something back, but it's too early, and we are miles away from happy things like toffee factories or the ocean. The radio's on, but I press a button. Something obvious about affection is then sung from her CD player, a portable rigged through the tape deck, little band stickers peeling off the edges, pictures of gramophones and singers with pompadours.

Outside, ladies walk dogs dressed in miniature ponchos. The rain falls and falls. We pass a schoolyard, its jungle gym and hobbyhorse all soaked and abandoned. When we pass other cars, our tires and their tires swap raspberries of street water. Rain is made of water and blame. Okay. You've seen rain before. Let's not get carried away. We can see the pitch of things just fine.

Allison's short. I don't know how this affects her eyesight. Her feet barely reach the pedals, but her bangs fall over her eyes and look nice.

"How many stickers have you gone through?" I ask, pointing to the CD player.

She shrugs. "We get them at the station."

"If I were you I would wear them on my cheek."

She sighs and looks at her nose in the mirror. "You shouldn't smoke in the shower."

"Look," I say, rolling up one sleeve. But Allison actually looks at me, a stare that makes me feel like sneezing. "Clint Eastwood does it," I whisper. "I read that somewhere. It feels great. I didn't mean to hurt you." I go to touch one of her tissues and she flinches. "What's that called? Why your nose did the thing."

"You know I don't—" she flicks her hand. "I don't function properly or whatever."

At her home the counter space is dominated by marinara stains and stray pills. While I'm busy stealing vanilla pretzels from the bulk bins, she ransacks the General Nutrition. She needs it all. Or supposedly needs. We dealt with needs this morning, bickering in her shower. I gave one dramatic puff and her nose started to bleed. Ding. Her point.

Here's life, somewhere in its own marginalia. But I feel glued to a lawn chair in the middle of a football stadium, like my afternoon won't end and all are witness. Right now I work at a greeting card shop downtown, a Victorian hut for the tourists, where in the back I paste glitter and install those tapes that play when you open the cards.

But that's not my thing. My thing is murals. For a guy whose handiwork covers the town, I am not super welcome. I mean, those in charge love my murals. So do tourists. Those who choose, however, to live here— to raise their kids, save coupons, hang lights—they just rub their eyes and sigh. But shit: mine are pretty tasteful. A wooden bridge in 3D on the abandoned bank building, now a bingo hall. A B-52 bomber on the side of the old library, now best assessed as a rat nook. My specialties are perspective and compliance. If the town restoration committee wants straw barrels and farm boys, here I be.

No, my murals are fine. My uncle, he was the one who slapped up the shockers. And fast too. You wouldn't guess from their detail how quick he worked. The 1860s townscape that sprawls into a peyote hippie wonderland? Two weeks. The wagon hold-up with Indians, cowboys, samurai and astronauts? Four. Painted on the chamber of commerce building. He used a lot of tarps, so nobody anticipated the extent of the damage.

Why did he fuck them up? He was bored, maybe, or high. I'm not prepared to call my uncle an artist. Yet every so often a man walks to work wearing lipstick. Getting noticed is easy. Some of us want to be remembered. Like you, maybe. Me, I want to be amused and loved a bit, modestly so. Every other day is fine. But my uncle—he wanted a psychedelic wagon robbery. The town awoke to see the fruit of this want and gave a collective *um*.

But people around here don't get ashamed. They don't. They just grow beards and hope for a thicker rain. My grandfather stood and doffed his cowboy hat at the city council meeting where they finally fired his son. He said, "I remember this town had a real thing for astronauts." That's what I hear, anyway. I didn't go. Apparently my grandfather made such a fuss that the council agreed to give our family another shot. Hi. My name's Another Shot.

It's not like we need the murals anymore. Blueberries are the new fad, good for memory, with marionberries right behind. So "people" from California have begun to move here, opening fusion restaurants and comfortable sweater outlets. But when the town first hired my uncle, times were dry. Old-fashioned boutiques and drugstores had long since bellied up. We were sad enough that any lame-ass antique vendor with a John Wayne lunchbox could snag a storefront. So the city council approved the restoration committee's big spirit project and put my uncle on the payroll. Disney had just fired him, caught him selling anatomically correct illustrations of famous cartoons. Mickey Mouse and Donald Duck: compromised. Our family tried to hide all this. Sure.

He showed up and started painting the summer before last, lived for a while between our couch and kitchen table, and would not explain to me the psychology of cartoon porn. "I could tell you it takes all kinds," he said, "but I'm more about sticking with the job. You pay me to draw anything and I'm keeping my mouth shut."

On his last mural, after the termination announcement, he ended up painting in the middle of a storm. Rain like nobody's business, wind rocking the ladder. The story goes that some punk kids rolled by and threw soda cans at him. Well, of course, one can caught him in the ankle and he "tripped." Then he demanded compensation pay. And the city, far from cutting him loose, ended up keeping him in style. "Sure I hammed the fall," he told me. "But the water does get me down. What if everything washes off? Hell, think about the guys who paint fire hydrants."

"They probably make inmates paint them," I said. He was showing me how to mural. This in our family's kitchen, him seated, leg in a cast. We were drinking Irish coffees and ruining my mother's wall.

"Prisoners," he said. "But prisoners get out. And then they see all this painting they did, washing off."

"Okay, what about masons? Stones rot."

My uncle took a sip of coffee, licked his cream mustache. "Paint's a beast of a different hair, as they say. Paint's—did anybody ever tell you how to hold a gun?"

"This is gonna be stupid."

"You hold it like it's an 'extension of your hand.'" He made the scare quotes with his fingers. "Paint, well. Paint is like an extension of your blood."

I didn't say anything. I started to paint a red cow on the wall.

"Reid, if you take this job, you're a real asshole."

"I'm in a good place right now," I said.

"What do you do?" my uncle said. "You get to be the mural guy. You're the mural guy. You get old, your kid's off somewhere fucking a dolphin trainer. What? It's the first thing I thought of. I'm not done. So you get old, and you hire up your kid's friend to replace you, and you die. Before that, they put your name on the ledger. You marry, what, twice? Twice."

"There's no ledger," I said. "It's just a town."

He shrugged. "Word to the wise. That's all."

My cow was a mess. "Cows aren't red," I said.

"It's your cow," my uncle said.

And when I had to clean it all up—by myself—I smelled like turpentine for three days. Sure I took the job. But it didn't pay enough, hence the greeting card gig. Allison thinks the murals are funny but a little boring. Sometimes I'll wake up thinking of them and smoosh my face in the pillow. But it's true about the rain. My uncle got that right. He was fired last October, and I've been muraling ever since. Whenever it rains, I find myself wiping the glitter off my sleeves and taking a smoke break. I wander down the street to one of my "scenes." Next thing I know, I've been standing for twenty minutes, teeth full of filter paper. It's worry. Half the worry of the crop watcher and half a weakness of the gut.

આ

"He fucked McJagger," Allison says, pointing.

A young dude is walking down the sidewalk ahead of us, thumb out. He's wearing a sleeveless t-shirt with a picture of David Bowie above the words I FUCKED MCJAGGER. Somewhere along the line, he lost his pants. Now he's trying to hitch in briefs and combat boots.

"I bet he's one of those punk kids," Allison says. "With the police car."

They angst around town, driving an outdated police car they bought at an auction. Sometimes they hop boxcars and joyride to the next town, leaving our Union Pacific rail workers even more depressed than they already are.

"What a loser," I say.

"Somebody should give him a ride," Allison says.

"That would ruin his whole thing. Like anarchy for life and everything. Now this, see this?" I put my hand on my heart. "This is about how we are all very fucked."

Allison smiles and slows. We stop a little past him, so he jogs to catch up. I lean over to unlock the backseat and glare at Allison.

The punk flops in. His legs are pasty but sturdy-looking. He rubs his hair—a tangerine-colored white boy 'fro—with both hands. "Fuck yes. I totally owe you." He wipes a hand on his boot and offers it up. "Luke."

Allison says her name and smiles and taps his fingers.

Luke points to his nose. "You've got a thing there."

Allison checks her tissue. "It's up there all right."

I give Luke's hand a shake. "I'm heavenly," I say. "You drive a police car."

"Man, that's not my—" He frowns. He starts to knead an invisible ball of dough, or that's what it looks like. "That, you know, that is more of a group mobile." He keeps kneading. "This is sort of the shape of car I would drive."

"Do you like omelets?" Allison asks.

I whisper things under my breath.

"Oh," Luke says. Then, after a while, "I don't have any money." He points at himself in the rearview. "And the pants. They're in a barn."

"Happens to the best of us," Allison says.

Luke leans forward. "Man," he says. "Man, I don't mean to put you out. If you had something going on this morning—"

I shrug. "Morning? What morning?"

Allison starts the car. I ask Luke if he's got enough leg room, then I click the seat back a few notches. He straightens, crosses his legs and picks at his lip with his nails. "You're gonna want to turn around," he says.

As we drive past everything we just saw, I lean close to Allison. "If this were a movie," I whisper.

"Yes, if."

"If this were a movie right now, I would push a button. Right here, here's where the button would be. And then a fireproof screen would go up between him and us, and I would ask you a lot of questions like what the fuck and variations on what the fuck."

"That's rich, Reid."

"You want me to offer our new friend a cigarette?"

She looks away from the road and runs a stare over me, like looking for the sock in the clutter, but she won't meet my eyes. "What's that mean?" I ask. "What are you doing?"

"I was trying to remember something." A car next to us. Slur of water. Gone.

"Well, did you?"

She ignores me. She grabs her CD case and drops it behind her into Luke's lap. He opens his eyes. "Pick something," Allison says.

❦

We met over interrogation. This summer I stood on a ladder in the parking lot behind the new library, painting a horse trailer for the annual parade. When I felt a tremble and looked down, I saw a girl in a blue fedora, squinting up and frowning. Oh. Me, of course, in Huck Finn overalls. I checked to make sure none of my teeth were missing.

"You're Reid," the girl said. "The celebrity. I have to interview you."

"Did I win something?"

"Well, you get to be interviewed by me," she said, smiling.

When Allison was a kid, her father delivered sturdy handshakes and worked for Clear Channel. Then he split, left his family and took the hair gel. Now Allison works at a community radio station. She's the manager and the only one paid. She wanted me for her local focus feature.

The interview didn't start so hot. I climbed down, and Allison held her nose the whole time at the paint smell. She apologized, but all her questions came out like "How blong iv you vin peighning?" It was cute. Endearing, even.

On our first date, this mix still threw me off: professionally endearing. Everything she said I agreed with, which was too much for her. She excused herself. Entirely. I didn't know what to do with her piece of pie, so

I gave it to a man sleeping outside in a shopping cart.

But something kept us running into each other. She called me to pick her up from a party. I borrowed her phone outside the movie theatre. One Sunday in July, we walked two miles deep into the park and found a rope swing. Then I began to spend the night. For breakfast, we would stumble down to this Greek diner for eggs and falafels. I figured out when to smile and when to scoff. For a while.

One day I helped her at the station with a group of third graders. We showed them knobs, let each one introduce a song. After they left, we went down to the basement where the station keeps all of their donations: records, broken ghetto blasters, a few extra didgeridoos from the group who sells them at the Farmer's Market. Somebody had even donated an old car seat. It smelled like you might think. God alone understands the motives of small town donors.

We sat on the car seat. Pretty soon we weren't really sitting. We used all the space the car seat would give. After, Allison drifted her finger along my stomach. "Let's move to Portland."

I nodded. I looked at all the walls of obscure vinyl, burnouts, imports, one-hit wonders. "We should do that," I said.

"Right," she said. "We should."

The room had a leak.

"Well," Allison said finally. "They don't have a heater down here do they?"

"Are you cold?"

"It's more like climate exposure. I can't be exposed too long."

I smiled and kissed her shoulder. "You look a little exposed." Allison turned her head against the arm of the car seat. Her bangs fell over her face. The room, meanwhile, continued to drip, leaking all over the donations and the one-hit wonders.

☙

Mud in your shoes is no fun. We're squishing through a field toward a barn. Luke's up ahead, hugging himself as he runs. Thanks to my consideration, I remembered to grab an umbrella. It keeps threatening to blow inside out. Allison stays close as we walk, brushing my hip and making me feel like we just met.

After following Luke's directions onto weed-pocked roads, we parked alongside some trampled chicken wire. Now we're up in the hills behind town, past even the R/V park.

When we got out, I pointed at the fence. "You can clear that?" I asked Allison.

She looked at me. "It's not a carnival ride, Reid."

Luke tried to slide under it, shove it up so we wouldn't have to climb over. This didn't work, only made him filthier, and Allison wouldn't take my offer of a boost. Her tissue fell out when she climbed over. But she plucked it up, twisted the shreds and shoved it all back in.

The tissue falls out twice more as we muck toward the pants barn. Every time this happens I stand there swinging the umbrella, trying a new stance. Rain pins Allison's bangs against her forehead. Like everyone who needs to talk, we don't.

At the barn, we find Luke huddled at the bottom of a stairwell, his head drooping. He keeps opening and closing his mouth. Allison touches his shoulder.

"Up here," he says, without raising his head. "Up the stairs."

"You live in a barn?" I ask.

"We were having a little shindig." He runs up the stairs and disappears inside.

I close the umbrella. Allison rests her head on my chest.

"Barns have hay," she says. "Am I allergic to hay? Hay fever?"

"Not all barns have hay," I say.

"I thought barns were just hay storage units."

"Barns can be very sacred places. Listen." I'm about to point out how this was her idea. Instead, I say, "We don't even have to stay."

"I think we have to stay. I don't know."

"Is your nose better?"

She looks up at me and smiles. "There's a lot of little crusty things. Little flakes. Like burnt sausage."

"Thank you for trying to make me feel better about missing breakfast." I touch the tip of her nose. "I was going to buy you breakfast."

Allison sighs, runs her hand across my chest and down my arm and gives me a little shove, shaking her head. Then she turns and walks up the stairs. I tap the banister with my umbrella, and I watch her climb closer to the rain.

ↄ৲

"The point of me replacing you," I said, "is that I replace you."

My uncle and I were parked across the street from the chamber of commerce watching men in orange vests sandblast the last of his murals. Every now and then, one of the workers would take his thermos, unscrew the lid, and splash liquid on a splotch of mural still left. He'd rub with his thumb, and even from across the street you could tell he was giggling.

My uncle sneezed. His leg cast was gone, but he had a cold and wore a yellow trench coat two sizes too big, even though this was the middle of October, Indian Summer and warm. "You need to see what really happens to these things," he said.

"Maybe I'm way off base, but I don't think any of the murals I paint will cause the restoration committee to host a bake sale at Round Table for the sole purpose of raising enough money to sandblast my art."

"Your art."

"I didn't want to say murals again."

"You're fine for the *job*, you can put some lines together, but—" He shook his head.

I sighed and looked at him. "So teach me that part, O wise one."

"Wisdomly advice," he said. He nodded and shut his eyes. "Wisdomly advice, wisdomly advice," he chanted. "Wisdomly wisdomly wisdomly wisdomly."

"Okay," I said. "I get it."

But he kept chanting. Thrust out his arms like a zombie and swayed his body. The sandblasters across the street got louder, but my uncle just upped the volume of the chant. Even when he stopped to cough and hock something and wipe his nose on his sleeve and I thought he was done, he wasn't. He started again, even louder.

"Are you okay?" I finally shouted.

Zip. Silence. Just the sandblasters. Then he opened his eyes, blinked once, and laughed. He laughed a couple more times, phlegmy barks. "You're headed for the ledger," he said. He crossed his arms. "Straight for it."

I looked away from him and started the car. "You only did it for the check, right?"

He let his arms fall. "I bought it, man. I believed in it. But I don't need it anymore. Me," he pointed to himself, "I'm not planning on dying. Okay? So no more paint for me."

I looked at him to see if he was serious, but I couldn't tell anymore.

"But knock yourself out," he said. "Paint's the worst thing to watch. Worst thing to go. Me, I'm not worried. One-way ticket to forever-ville. Right here."

"Sounds boring."

"If I was the only one left?" He tugged both of his long, floppy sleeves over his hands, so he looked armless. He stared at his lap. "If I'm the only one left, then who can I fucking bore?"

We drove away from the chamber, past the bingo hall, drove until the town road met the freeway exits. Then up the onramp, past the restoration committee's levee beautification project, for which they were bulldozing the trees near the bridge to plant smaller, more exciting trees. No one has ever been bored to death the way they've been stoned to death, or starved. Doesn't happen.

In his epic yellow coat, my uncle stared out the window. Every couple of seconds he sniffed. "Towns are really weird little thing," he said suddenly. "I don't think humans invented them. The same humans who fuck each other and don't want to look? They didn't invent towns. Towns must be a space alien thing."

I laughed, but he didn't.

"If you're about to stay somewhere," he said, "don't. If your bed doesn't have any wheels, go ahead and paint 'em on."

Green flanked the freeway, and pumpkin-colored leaves. Oregon in the autumn—look it up. It's something. I drove and stared and tried to account for things in terms of what would last, whose work and how long, and what kind of work might fool you into believing too hard.

∽

What about carpenters? Ants, termites: bad news for wood. I wish my uncle were here to see the seven billion ants marching in a whirlpool around the mouth of an apricot brandy bottle.

Luke comes over and stares with me. He's found a pair of blue, pinstriped trousers. But the knees are blown out, so they're still cred-worthy, I guess.

"There's a lot of sugar in that stuff," he says.

I nod. "They know what they like."

Aftermath themes the barn. Cans of PBR everywhere, forties too, a few boxes of wine. Orange and white cigarette butts scattered like a new strain of wildflower. Stains cover three lumpy couches: a paisley couch, a sweet corn white, and some ugly brown mishmash, all still upright. Another couch, a purple loveseat, sits upside-down with springs exposed. Above us is a loft and up in the barn's A-framed eves hangs a disco ball, swaying with pitters of technicolor shine as the rain slogs the roof. Poor Allison. Beneath the beer and hangover sweat, it does smell like hay.

Luke kicks the brandy bottle, shipwrecking the ants. He puts his hand on the small of my back. "You want anything to eat? We have peanut butter and stuff."

"Where's Allison?"

Luke looks at me.

"The girl I was with."

"Oh. She's in the kitchen."

"Kitchen?"

"The owner people converted it. It's up in the loft. They don't really use this for a barn barn, you know?"

I dodge everything as best I can, heading upstairs to the kitchen. There I find Allison standing over a plastic card table where a few more punks have landed, two sleeping spooned beneath—boy and girl, I think, mohawks limp and spike belts undone—and one leaning back in a metal chair.

Allison dabs at the leaning guy's eye with a piece of her tissue. I feel like I've missed something. She motions me over. "Reid, we need your opinion. Does he really look like a Seamus?"

The guy on trial looks like he could hack a mosh pit, but he's no Irish warlord. Isn't that Seamus? Like a Shamrock Genghis Kahn? I don't know my history. This Seamus is a waif, left eye bruised and pink. He wears a bandanna loose around his neck and holds a mandolin. He plucks a couple strings and grins at me, half yawns.

"He looks like Billy Idol," I say to Allison.

Seamus nods. "No doubt."

Luke walks in. "Seamus," he says, "you are more or less the shittiest host ever." He kicks aside a couple beer boxes and opens a blue cooler in the corner, tossing Alison and me two cans of frozen orange juice concentrate. I sort of stare at mine, but Allison laughs.

"Yeah," Luke says. "Yeah." He wanders back out.

"There's probably some tequila somewhere," Seamus says. "Well, no. I don't know why I said that. There isn't. What time is it?"

"We should go," I say. "It's almost noon."

"Shit," Seamus says, hugging his mandolin. "That's like—I never even went to sleep."

"Do you have a bathroom?" Allison asks. Seamus points to what I thought was a broom closet, then Allison's gone.

What am I supposed to do now? Fix the sink? Thumb wrestle somebody? I lean against the fridge and hit the orange juice can against my palm.

"So you live here?" I say.

"Just got back into town," Seamus says. "I was down around New Orleans, building houses and stuff."

Trust me, I don't want to talk. I'm wet and unwilling to respect the valuable soul of this young man staring at my boring haircut. I want my mouth to grow and grow until I can gulp up Seamus and his whole sorry crew and spit their ridiculous police car in front of a semi. Let me be honest: my town is full of kids like Seamus. But not of—

She's out, shaking her hands dry. "Really?" she says. "Was it with a church or something?"

"A group," Seamus says. "Some group. I don't know. There was actually—" he laughs. "Okay, there was actually this girl who came through town—"

"Oh there was," Allison says, giving him a look.

"Coming back from there, yeah, talking about it, and she was going back and—" he stops and shrugs. Allison nods, smiles coy. I turn around and open the fridge and press my can of orange juice very hard into a half-open stick of butter and then I take out my can and close the fridge.

"She got tetanus," Seamus says. "Had to leave. But I stayed there through summer. Put the tract houses together and walked around Bourbon Street and shit." He starts to play something on the mandolin. "This black guy, we were working on his old street, and he sat around and watched us.

When we finished up, he gave me a harmonica."

"Oh," Allison says. "I thought you were going to say he gave you the mandolin."

"Luke gave me the mandolin," Seamus says. He points to his black eye. "And this."

Maybe Luke's okay after all.

"Then!" Luke yells, popping into the kitchen so quick I drop my umbrella. "This fucker got kicked out of the program and moved back."

I stare at him. He holds an electric razor, cord dangling. "Your head," I say.

"My head." He puts a hand there, where his orange 'fro is adios. Gone. Now the scalp is only fuzz and nicks, some of which are definitely still bleeding.

"Oh my God," Allison says.

Seamus nods. "I like it."

Allison tears another piece from her tissue then sees that won't do much good. One of the punks under the table stirs and gives a little squeal.

I pick up my umbrella. "We really need to go."

"Wait," Luke says. Buzz cut blood dribbles onto his ear. "You guys were nice enough to—you should see the train."

Seamus leaps up. "The train!" He toes the people under the table, but they're conked out, so he grabs Allison's hand and tries to take off. But she holds his grip and stays put, which flings Seamus like a minor ballet partner into the side of the fridge. He crumples. Luke laughs. And bleeds. Allison slaps her hand over her mouth and points down. "Reid," she says. So I drop the umbrella again and crouch and slap Seamus on the back, like I'm burping him, but he just groans. "Let him breathe," Allison says. "You're not doing it right."

I stand and blink. "How am I supposed to *let* him breathe?"

"You're not doing it right," she says again.

Luke looks at Seamus and shakes his head. He chucks the razor, swipes a beer can off the floor, goes over to the sink, and fills the can with water. Then he dumps the water on Seamus's head. He does this a couple more times. I move by Allison and try to put my hand under her hair, but she twists away. Finally Seamus lurches up, nudges a fist at Luke and manages to bat away the can. Luke seizes him and lifts him and sets him down on his feet. They embrace like this, Seamus hunched over, Luke's chin resting on his back, smiling like he's on whatever he's probably on. I can hear Allison breathe next to me, and I imagine that I'm breathing along, but neither of us checks to make sure.

"Shit," Seamus said, coughing. "I guess you don't like trains."

"He's kind of a dick scrubber," Luke says. "But it is a cool train."

"Allison," I say. "Do you want to go?"

"I don't know."

I turn to look at her, and she stares at me with that mangled tissue crammed up her nose. Everything she's said all morning has been inflected with a trace of nasal block, that sitcom nerd voice. Should I have mentioned this sooner? Made a joke? But that's one mercy I understand. We never call the people we love on the things they can't do anything about. But they just wish we would tell the truth.

"Tell me the truth," I say. "You want to go see this train thing? I'm not even hungry anymore."

"Not here," Allison says. "I don't want to talk about this here."

"Let's go then." I pick up the umbrella. "Let's move to Portland. You and me."

Allison turns to Seamus and Luke. "He's kidding," she says. "That's what he does when he's scared. He makes a joke."

"You're right." I draw a line in the air with the umbrella. "Here are the cowards over by me, and you're all the brave little cub scouts. And the community radio stations. You're all the community radio stations helping out God's own motherfucking community."

Allison snatches the umbrella from my hand. "The only people who are ever going to do anything with their life are the ones too fucked up to worry about it."

"Luke didn't want me to go," Seamus says. He wrestles out of Luke's hug and stumbles a little. "He was like boo-hoo, what if it floods again?"

"He can't swim," Luke says.

Allison looks at me. Her eyes are tender and exhausted. "And here you are, worried about my goddamn nose."

She pulls out the cotton. Blood starts to snake down her face. It drips, rivers, joins a wine stain. Such a large amount of blood for a short girl's nose.

"Hold on," I say, because I want to do it right this time.

But she shakes her head and keeps shaking. She drops the umbrella. Allison. Laughing. Rope swing. Falafel. Car seat. Garlic. I'm just trying to think of the right way to do this. Her face is right there, and it could be any girl who stumbled into a barn full of punks and had her nose punched in the revelry, but it's not.

She leaves, blood all the way.

And I want to chase her, but I want the starter's gun to backfire. And I want to forget her, boom, but I want to cook her breakfast, dedicate the whole idea of breakfast to her. One time I woke up and found myself alone in the bed, and I thought well, that was fun while it lasted, but that thought was kind of a lie. And then I found her in the kitchen doing something with a griddle, a box of pancake mix, and a counter full of apples. She was singing British rock songs with a fake accent. I told her I was stupid. She turned around to see me and said yes. Then I told her she was stupid. She turned the burner off and kissed me on the neck.

"We are all very fucked," I say. I place my hand on my heart. Just to try it out. Should I be this stuck? Have I signed up for life already? My uncle's right. People build towns to come together out of the rain, and all the rest of it—the bingo halls, the restoration committees—that's like a joke you tell to keep your mouth awake, so you can talk certain people into staying.

"Who's fucked?" Seamus says. I look up and the two of them are still there. For some reason I thought they'd freeze, but they exist, of course, way outside my stupid heart. Seamus taps a red pack against his palm, and Luke has a cigarette tucked behind his ear.

"We missed the train," Luke says.

"Isn't there a next one?" I ask.

Luke nods and looks as thoughtful as anyone wearing an I FUCKED MCJAGGER shirt can get. "We'll walk slow," he says.

Out we go, back under the rain. No sign of Allison. They lead me steeper into the woods. We head through a mess of pine trees and fir trees and thorn weeds, which tear a gash in Luke's MCJAGGER shirt. As the trees multiply and bunch closer, the sound of the rain dulls and the only evidence left is the wet droop of a leaf or a bright moss. I try to call Allison. No signal. We walk through the trees until they begin to thin some, rain again audible, and then we hit a clearing.

At first, I don't understand. What I see are strange black cylinders. Then I get it. Tires. Tires upon tires upon tires. So many I can't process them at first. Tractor tires, semi tires, car tires. Towers of tires and tire huts. Tires sawed in half and strips of tire bark, tires sinking into mud and dandelions, and tires stacked too high about to topple over. Rain thuds against the rubber and pools in the grooves. It smells like the inside of a Halloween mask. And through the middle of all this, bordered by bicycle tires, runs a set of train tracks.

"Jesus," I say.

"We stole them," Luke says.

"We moved them," Seamus says. "We moved them when the town wanted to build that new park by the river. They hired a few of us to clean up everything, but we just took all these tires and put them in some trucks."

"Who throws tractor tires in a river?"

Luke gallops over to a stack and scrambles up. He balances one-footed atop the stack and screams.

Seamus offers me a cigarette. I bite my lip but decline.

"If there's one thing I learned in the South," Seamus says, "it's don't ask why people throw shit in a river."

He wanders over to Luke's tire perch, and Luke passes him a lighter. Seamus struggles a little against the wind but gets it. Then he holds up his cigarette and Luke holds his down and they share tips.

I crouch in the dirt and feel pretty safe here. A kid again. Before I dumped glitter for a living and worried about Allison or murals or any of that. If you let me just sit here for a little while, I'm sure I'll figure something out. Or maybe I'll sit until the tires elect me mayor. Until they print the ledger.

Later that day, I will come home for a free dinner to find my uncle split. My parents will tell me how he lurched in at three a.m. How he took a carton of milk from the fridge, tried to make a White Russian. Then he took the milk into the living room, turned on the TV, fell asleep in front of a late night NASCAR rerun, and spilled the entire carton across the coffee table. If he owes you any money, my father will tell me, kiss it off. But he doesn't. He owes this world squat. You know people like that, don't you? All their badass distance from the flock finally catches up to them. If he does die, I won't attend the service. I'll pay some neighborhood kid to rob the flowers off his plot. Someone's bound to buy flowers; the graveyard beautification committee will insist. And I will pay that kid even more to eat them.

"Not me," I tell Seamus. "They wouldn't throw me in the river."

He sort of laughs like, *Look boys, we've got a live one.* "Totally," he says. He and Luke share an eye roll. They think I'm the boringest fuck. Then Luke's brows raise and he jumps off his tire stack. "I'm not a dog," he says. "But tell me if you don't hear that."

We do. A rumble.

Low and far, like years away, and then in a double-take the train's upon us. The horn bawls. Boxcars racket past, gray and maroon rusted iron. Some of the cars black stamped by Cyrillic or Chinese letters, others numbered. Double-stacked well cars, cars straight from World War II, and long tanker cars with dents in the metal that glint when the rain meets them. On almost all of the cars is some daze of graffiti, names you can't even make out.

"What does that say?" I yell.

"Dude," Seamus yells. "You're not supposed to read it."

Luke runs up to the track and cups his hand around his mouth. But the train is gone before he can ask anything, before he even has a chance.

Restart? Restore?

They retired for a while then for real. Orrin sold the lawnmower and Rhonda bought emergency flashlights. Catalytic heaters and a macerator pump. They didn't buy the R/V official until Nevada, what for tax schemes. They canceled subscriptions and sold furniture, said that Rand McNally would handle their funerals. They dressed the same but changed backdrops. Fall in Vermont and winter in New Mexico. They boondocked their R/V in the parking lots of Wal-Marts and tribal casinos. They parked in schoolyards, on private game preserves, at shooting clubs. Flea markets, gun shows, pottery festivals. When they passed near the family, they stayed with the family. But mostly they stayed on proper R/V sites, the best in Wyoming and the worst in New Jersey. Orrin screwed the blue sewage snake into hole after hole, Rhonda tested the flush, and Orrin yelled back "Are we shitting in cotton yet?" Once they saw a family of sparrows in a laundromat parking lot. A gang fight near a Motel Six. Ozarks and redwoods. Both oceans and one gulf. They kept their Pomeranian, sprinkled Dramamine in his puppy hash when he got skittish in the Rockies. Orrin unrolled the awning with a crankshaft; Rhonda set the paper plates on the fold-out card table. Orrin complained about the wireless signal; Rhonda scouted for milk stores. They drank iced tea near lakes. They ate campfire suppers with other R/V couples. Chatted with Civil War buffs and retired crop dusters. Rhonda bought a backpack violin, but she only ever learned to pluck. When Orrin spiked · his Pepsi, he'd get to talking about the ghost of Dwight Eisenhower, about the interstate—anything built so long you forget how it started and just stare. All of this Orrin shared in emails. The family got Orrin's emails and did stare. Out the window: trains and persimmon trees, pick-up baseball in the park across the street. The family waited for Orrin's emails or didn't. The family saved Orrin's pictures or deleted them for space. Must be nice, the family said. When are you coming home, the family said. Rand McNally, Orrin said. Better ask him.

ↄ⋰

When Rhonda died, Orrin parked the rig at his daughter's house in Reno. Being Orrin's baby brother, I could foresee the bounce around plan. Soon as winter passed, he aimed west: the coast, Crescent City, our driveway. My wife dusted everything, even the salt shaker, which struck me as a little wonkish.

"What, that make the food taste better?" I said.

"Clean is clean," she said "It eases a person."

After she was done, I grabbed the shaker. "Uh oh," I said. "Fingerprints."

She sat down across the table from me and massaged a flat hand with a fist, a kind of mortar and pestle. There's four chairs. Our daughters both did the college thing: Gale for forestry and Leigh for acting, both away and burrowed now in very different setups. Unlike Orrin, they don't feed us much news. Worry's always there, but it's dwarfed by wondering. Of every twenty daydreams we have about our daughters, we confess maybe two. The rest come at red lights, over tuna salad, watching reporters in flimsy ponchos. We're just anybodies: only when there's no talk do our thoughts blend together.

"You should fix that scooter," my wife said. "Vroom vroom."

"He'll be fine," I said. "He'll have some way of getting around."

"What if they drive him in?"

I've converted our daughters' bedroom to a workshop. Woodworking, disemboweling smoke alarms. "More fiddling," my wife calls it, alluding to the antique typewriters on the porch and the shed full of crippled transportation like the moped I've been coaxing for years. I went to the bedroom and got my toolbox, came back to the kitchen. "Day that guy doesn't drive himself is the day wheels turn square."

My wife was still at the table. She took the salt shaker and set it sideways. She flicked, and the shaker rolled across and off. If any salt spilled, you couldn't see.

"Might take me all day," I said.

"Holler if you need anything."

"Well into the night."

She got up and found a sponge. Opened the microwave and set about scraping some char. "Your eyes hurt when you're in there too long. Wear your glasses."

I went to the fridge and rooted around. My wife came over, reached past me and grabbed a package of cheese singles, put it in my hand. I kissed her wrist before she pulled it away.

In the shed, I gave up on the moped after the usual pokes. Then I started remixing fuel for my R/C plane. It's a standard little two-stroke glower, despite my best efforts to install the motor off my weed whacker. I used funnels and jugs, pouring and capping and shaking. Methanol and castor oil, other stuff I have to mail order. Lamps stayed off because of the nitromethane, and in the dark I thought about the last time Orrin visited, when we took the plane for a whir in the cliffs above Enderts Beach. He was giddy to steer in all that wind. Kept saying the ocean wouldn't mess with the two of us. "Don't fret, kiddo," he said, "we're keeping this puppy bone dry." Both of us collect pensions, but I'm still kiddo. After the fuel was mixed, I soldered random stuff and let remembrance work me over: Orrin getting a pompadour and our dad throwing a fit; Orrin sharking me and every other sucker at eight ball; Orrin fixing to drag race the night of '64's tsunami. He used to break into the Battery Point Lighthouse and bring girls, winking them out of clothes and into trouble. Of course it was me getting my toys ready for him. My mortgage paid off.

Never moved away. Married local. It'll be me in a suit and him in a box. Me with a speech full of his name. Which does make me wonder. In our conversations since Rhonda passed, he's been the chipper one. "Don't fret, kiddo." Like the plane's in the sand but he's still steering away, laughing at the sky. But what if it's not my plane we're talking about? What if it's his plane? And what if the ocean won't give up? What if we're not really talking about a plane?

❦

Okay, so Dad warned me about his dog's poops but not about the smell. They're sneaky little stinks. We find these pellets of Pomeranian shit behind cushions, in slippers, you name it. Dad acts embarrassed, sure, but only in that way of his. "Can't say he's much for domesticating," he says, letting the dog lick his chin and yap like a tea kettle. "Really more of a miniature wolf here."

My boyfriend loves it. When he finds the shit, he yells "Inspection!" Orrin's got him pie-eyed and saying golly. Used to be my dad wanted to scare my boyfriends. Now he wants to buddy up. I can't decide which gives me the bigger headache. Luckily, he's only staying until spring, then he's off to my uncle's in California. I bet he thinks he's borrowing our car, and the shit of it is that he's probably right.

One thing that's nice is me and my boyfriend forget to bicker. Orrin takes him to dirt car races and roller derbies. I stay home and take online classes. Me and my boyfriend, we made these pacts to "better our situations." And believe me, we yell about those quotation marks. My boyfriend loafs from casino job to casino job; can't even hold one at the factory that *makes* the goddamn slot machines. Me, I work for Amtrak, and it's all I can do not to tell every drunk rancher streaming in with camouflage and cheesy goatees to get right back on the train. Nobody's scraping happy times in Reno. So having Dad around that first week or two was a swell break, sure.

Bright, zany. Especially since he was trying so hard, trying not to dwell on Rhonda. But pretty soon it was like ugh, enough.

One night he comes in the door with the dog balanced on a stack of pizzas. "We're gonna have a poker night," he says. "Gimme some phone numbers." The dog jumps and scurries.

"Nobody needs more poker," I say. "I'm studying."

"But this is the sort we can win," he says. He sets a greasy slab of pizza right in my lap, right where I've got a textbook open for nursing class. "I've got this feeling coming on," he says. "Let's call around. Five-card draw." He sits Indian style on the floor, rolling pizza slices into cigar shapes. "You got at least what, two friends?"

That's when my boyfriend enters, dripping in a towel. I swear, it's like my dad's got two puppies now. My boyfriend's hair is damp and spindly, looped behind his ears. Skin peach from scrubbing. Sure, he looks pretty good. Shake a stick. "What's all this talk about winning?" he says, doing some kind of John Wayne imitation, I think.

I snort. "Shootout at dumbass corral."

Dad laughs, eats a pepperoni. "Smart as a cayenne pepper. Always said so. Half the time I don't get what she means, but damn if I don't feel the heat."

My boyfriend sits next to me and grabs the pizza out of my lap. I shut my textbook and fling it at the radiator. Dad flinches. The dog runs over and starts climbing the book: slipping, climbing, slipping, squishing the spine.

"Well, we will need to do some resource pooling," my boyfriend says.

I scoot away on the couch. "No. No poker."

"Whoa," my boyfriend says. He rests a wet leg across my knees. "Chill pill."

"If you need a little buy in," Dad says, "I can help out. It's not us we're out to swindle, right? It's them. Them all." He hooks a thumb toward the window. It's a musty little living room, TV tray for a coffee table, but Dad's still enough to catch you twice. All his teeth still white, his hair silvering like actors and windmills. Paul Newman. Sometimes, racing my shopping cart, I notice those expensive Newman cookies and imagine myself as that daughter behind Paul. Faking the farm life. In on the joke. Not that I'm the first girl to wish that. But Paul's always got an extra slump, a little looser than his daughter, you know? Go look at those cookies. Tell me who's having fun and who's doing the work.

"It's not that," my boyfriend says to my dad. "Though we appreciate it, definitely." He holds the pizza up. "Having you here, helping us out and all."

"Us?" I blurt. "He's helping *us*?"

"Easy now," my boyfriend says.

"It's not easy," I say. "What's easy about it?"

"Plenty of help," my boyfriend says.

"Well, I don't feel helped," I say.

My boyfriend frames his teeth like, *Whoa there, that's enough.* But I keep going. "And I'm sorry, but you know what? That dog. I'm sick of that goddamn dog. How long we supposed to serve that dog, huh? We've got situations. He's not helping our situation."

Even before I'm done, I'm seeing Dad's face and aching to shut up, but here's how I work with talking: leave it alone and I'm super. Otherwise, different story.

What Dad does is laugh and sigh. He shuts his eyes, rubs his jaw. Then he walks over and brushes my bangs off my forehead, real soft. Calls the dog, who scampers and trips on a lamp cord. Dad walks and leans against the front door and sort of strokes the knob. "Get dressed," he says to my boyfriend. He opens the door. "You're wet."

Dad spends the night in his camper, and my boyfriend mopes around, watching sitcoms on mute so all the laugh cues look like everybody's forgotten their lines. At least I get some work done. When I've uploaded my assignments, I get a jar of marshmallow fluff and a thing of Oreos and sit next to him. "Peace offering," I say.

He doesn't look at me. "I can take it. Fine. But it's not good for him to have you yelling and sniping like that. The man's wife just died. You want to talk about situations, but that's it for him. That's his whole life. And don't tell me to sit tight because it's not my dad or some shit. You know we're blind. When it comes to this shit? We're blind." He turns and points at me.

I open the fluff. There's no spoon, so I eat some with my fingers. Then—and I swear it's because I forgot the spoon, but tell somebody that and he'll say *yeah sure*, he'll claim he knows better, he'll start working to make things right when all you want is for the working to go away—I start to cry.

"Oh Jesus," my boyfriend says. He puts his finger down. "Baby, come on."

"I'm fine," I say, wiping my eyes and getting marshmallow on my face.

He takes me in a while. Then he says, "If I ever lost you."

"He's leaving," I say. "In March."

"When's March?"

"I don't know. Soon."

"Things'll be great by March," my boyfriend says, pulling me close. "March won't know what hit it."

And what I think, sitting close like that, is wouldn't this be a swell time to find one of the Pomeranian's little nuggets in the marshmallow? Right there in the no-name fluff on the TV tray. And my boyfriend could spot it while I blubber, and he could pluck it out, and some big ass LAUGHTER sign could go red. Does my Dad have a TV? Because he's got the computer, but I guess I've never been inside the motorhome long enough to notice a TV. And I think of him in there, alone. And I think of how we don't have the money, but maybe we should buy him a little set before he goes, before he takes off. Blinking my eyes clean, I peek in the jar.

Marshmallow, all marshmallow.

First thing he wanted to do was make us supper. I was right: he'd borrowed his daughter's station wagon. We drove with him for groceries. It was drizzling. "Jackalope stew," he said. "But we'll use beef. It's this Native American thing. Rhonda and me, we ate at this place in New Mexico—all adobe, real traditional. We got the recipe. Tradition says that guests get to pick one ingredient. And you're my guests, even though I'm your guest. Get it?" He grinned and steered with his knee.

From the backseat, my wife said, "Leigh drove through New Mexico once. Says that everything's clay. Even the phone booths."

"Painted desert," Orrin said. "Alien town."

I glanced at his face. Still a construction worker's ruddiness, tan blotching with age. What he's done all his life is build, conned himself a private backhoe and never looked back. Scuffed his boots all over. Rhonda was his second wife, and I always thought she was a sturdy thing for him. She could ride on the back of a motorcycle and still pack napkins. Orrin used to insist the R/V was her idea, really. If you're setting to move, she told him, let's move. Let's not pussyfoot around.

Orrin drove in the slow lane—didn't pass anybody, not even semis. Just putted along and squinted. That's one thing. He squinted a lot.

"Where's the dog?" I said.

Orrin shrugged. "Left him in Reno."

In the grocery store, my wife picked radishes and I picked mesquite potato chips. Orrin guffawed when I handed him the chips, started crunching the bag on the checkout belt. "Giving me all the hard work, kiddo," he said.

The stew was better than I expected, and my wife did dishes while Orrin and I fiddled with the electronic weather inspector on the porch. The porch is screened, and our view gets lots of Pacific, so you can sit and watch rain batter the bluffs and tides. Water working all the angles, gray to foam. But what I wanted to show Orrin was the inspector, which Gale got me for Christmas. It's like a miniature weather channel: green overlays float across a Monopoly-sized world map, and if you kink the antennas right, you've got yourself a look at precipitation in Tokyo. Even comes with a remote to aim should you want temperature, air pressure and so forth.

"Helluva gadget," Orrin said. "Watch this." He put the remote on his forehead. "I'm guessing—cold." Then he aimed at Greenland. The numbers went negative. He handed me the remote. "This thing ever conks out, you just call your big brother."

I smiled and unplugged the inspector. We sat in chairs and listened to all the water. Rainwater from outside, dishwater from inside. Orrin nudged one of my typewriters with his boot. "Appreciate your having me," he said. "I'm not planning on setting up shop or anything." He stretched and popped his knee. "Fact is, I'm scouting for a favor."

"Favor away."

He got up and rapped the window. Started a rhythm. Then he coughed and couldn't quit, had to spit. He sat again. "Need to drive down to Humboldt County," he said. "See my daughter-in-law, Deseree."

What was funny about him squinting, I realized, was that he's always mocked my glasses. When we were kids, he used to ask me for Buddy Holly's autograph and hide my glasses in the icebox. But if anybody else made fun, he'd beat their faces until they needed their own prescription.

"You want some company?" I asked.

"Something like that." He stared at the rain. "Something between a sidekick and a—" he stopped. "Hell, you tell me. Sidekick and a what?"

These days, my system can't handle much in the way of alcohol, but seeing Orrin's face, I badly wanted a bottle to give over. Instead, I grabbed an old bellcrank. Holding it out to Orrin, I sort of patted his hand closed around it. "Hermano," I said, embarrassed. "Saying it wrong, I bet, but that's how Miss Thompson taught us."

Orrin snorted and grinned. "Remember when I got detention for making fun of her hickeys? Spanish! The hell did she know about Spanish?"

"Not a Spanish bone in her body," I said. "Plenty of body, though." We laughed. Orrin tucked the bellcrank in his pocket, but it stuck out weird, and we doubled up on the laughter. I heard the sink stop, and I knew my wife would bring us coffee. We'd have a fine evening, the three of us. On Orrin's guest bed, the blankets smelled like lemons. That night I would tell my wife that Orrin and I were driving down to Humboldt for the weekend. Heads on pillows, we would do our thinking. Over Orrin, over our daughters. We'd speak of life as if it were everything between us and living. But it'll all work out, we'd say. It'll all work out. Then one of us would fall asleep first, which the other would know by their breathing. I'd leave with Orrin, and my wife would wait for me. That was a hell of a thing to know, that she'd do that. For a second, I couldn't even look at Orrin. We were still chuckling, but I couldn't meet his face. He was my brother, and I couldn't even take him in.

&

They dawdled at vistas. Deseree wasn't expecting them until evening, Orrin said. So they spent the day among poppies and crags, tourists and briny wind. They hit their headlights and drove through sequoia groves. They braked for guardrails feet from the ocean. They saw lagoons, Roosevelt elk, faded pastels and alpacas. Lighthouses and lumber companies. Cattle and hail. They talked of penny candy and bobcat scares. Childhood and politics. The encroachment of marijuana and the slickos in Sacramento. They argued about who'd gone to which movie with which girl. Which year this-or-that went belly up, which year so-and-so joined the Navy. Fog glommed over cliffs, suds lapped the sand. The 101 channeled them through Eureka, waterlogged art deco. They let the day swallow the drive. Outside of a giant blue ox, they parked and ate sandwiches. Orrin threw away his onions; his brother took a licorice digestion pill. They talked of milk and gas prices. They cozied into ancient jokes. When they saw wings, Orrin said vulture. His brother said hawk. Pretty soon they switched guesses. Orrin told whoppers; his brother whistled. Something would remind Orrin of an R/V story, and off he'd go. Yam yam. They jostled the station wagon through a drive-through tree: a fussily hollowed redwood flanked by a gift shop. We never managed to get the rig through this puppy, Orrin said. That's one thing we couldn't do, he said. His brother slapped him on the back. Cross that one off, he said. If St. Peter asks, Orrin said. Yes, sir, I'll say. Hell yes. They only had a few miles to go until Garberville, so they took the Avenue of the Giants. More redwoods. Splintered light. Ferns and stumps, trillium and sorrel, butterflies and a frock of damp. Something didn't agree with Orrin's stomach, so his brother drove. They'd been driving the Giants a few minutes when Orrin said, We did this road. We did this both ways. Rhonda wanted to drive through that tree, but we couldn't, so we turned and drove back the way we came. They drove in silence. They didn't try the radio. When they got back onto 101, they saw a hitchhiker: young man with a derby hat and dreadlocks, cut-off jean shorts and a backpack that dwarfed him. The sleeves of his Star Wars t-shirt were torn off. He held out his thermos for a ride. The brothers didn't slow. Night crept down around them. When they got into Garberville, Orrin nudged his brother. Check it out, he said, pointing. On a sign outside a bar was a neon cowgirl. She lit in stages. First her body, then her lasso, then her hat. Then backwards, until she disappeared. Orrin and his brother pulled into the bar's parking lot and idled. Body, lasso, hat. Hat, lasso, body. That tree, Orrin said. That goddamn tree.

From: Wade Hayworth <wade.hayworth@gmail.com>
To: Orrin Hayworth <orrrrrrrrrrin1967@comcast.net>

Subject: re: garbervile??

dear dad,

wow, hmm. honestly i dunno if that's a great idea. things between me and deseree didn't exactly end with a mountain of lollipops, and now she's taking care of this new dude's (gary? gary or gerry) kid, i think. why do you need to stay in garberville, anyway?? can't you stay with uncle brigham up in crescent city?? i know you always got along with deseree, but i don't think she drinks anymore, so it won't be like you remember. i guess i don't know if you drink anymore either.

i know you hate the city, but you can always visit here. portland doesn't really count as a city. it's like a noir movie with a high speed rail. and food at all the bars! there's this one bar you can get kobe beef sliders. you can even get aMURican food if you want. haha. ;) i know you said it was hard to drive the r/v around seattle, but i think portland might be easier, and maybe you can borrow tracey's car?? just gimme a weeks notice or whatever before you come up and we'll primetime for fun.

i'll try to give tracey a call one of these weekends. get her to patch me thru. things are crazy right now, but we're all busy these days, right? that's what days are for. i feel like we haven't really gotten a chance to really talk. about rhonda and everything. so i'd love to hear from you. i feel like it's always sort of weird for us, maybe, to talk straight, but i promise not to slip into joke mode if you promise too. i'm thinking about you and caring about you all the time. we all are. i mean, you're probably doing fine. but yeah. that's always been kind of weird to me, that equation, like if you're doing fine, people are supposed to say oh, okay, they're fine, check them off the care list.

anyway, gimme a buzz. send some reno pics. don't steal any old ladies' lunch money. you should get one of those dice necklaces. ha!

love,

wade

p.s. attached is deseree's contact info

⁊

We got to Deseree's trailer. There was a tricycle and a busted pumpkin. We killed the headlights and let the car guzzle for a little. Rain dripped from wind chimes. Some trailers were bright, but most, like Deseree's, were dark.

"I need to rinse my face," Orrin said. He put a hand on my knee. "Let's go easy on the Rhonda business in there. They never met."

"She ever meet Wade's mom?"

Orrin's smile was tired. "Well, you'd have to ask Wade."

Deseree answered the door in men's boxer shorts and a Sierra Nevada sweatshirt. She hugged herself and peered. "You guys religious or something?"

Orrin opened his cell phone under his face. The glow made him look like a too old trick-or-treater. Deseree saw his face, huffed, and poked his chest a couple times. "No shit," she said. "Damn me in a goddamn shit."

"Here for the sights," Orrin said. "Find 'em, haunt 'em, sign the guestbook."

Deseree laughed. Kind of a cross between a laugh and the word "ha." She walked past us, barefoot, and felt for rain.

Orrin hooked a thumb toward the trailer. "What's the word on codgers in there?"

"Sure, stay, come in," Deseree said. "But you need to park somewhere else."

"I can move it," I said.

Deseree looked at me and Orrin grabbed me in a bear hug. He tried to heft, but I didn't go anywhere. I stuck my hand to Deseree, my arm trapped by the hug. "Brigham. Orrin's brother."

She nodded. "Y'all got a hell of a family. Wolves'd be lucky to have a pack like yours."

Orrin let me go and walked to the car. He popped the trunk and pulled a six-pack of Pale Ales, holding them to Deseree. She shook her head and kissed him on the cheek. His shoulders eased. He tossed the beer back in the trunk. I was surprised, because I didn't remember him buying or stashing them. Deseree led him by the elbow into her trailer, but I stayed outside awhile, feeling more and more like a sailboat at a speedway. What did I even call her? My niece-in-law? Step-niece-in-law? Ex-step-niece-in-law? When you need that many dashes to explain why you're knocking on somebody's life—well, it was Orrin I was there for. Sidekick hermano. Which rings a little nicer: like a code name, like a superhero.

Trailers blend rooms, which makes it hard to think of them as homes. Where's the den end, I mean. When there's a stack of celebrity biographies and medieval figurines on a table that's sitting half carpet, half linoleum, would you call that table coffee or kitchen? It's a manner of living that unnerves me. On Deseree's couch was a pallet of clementines. Orrin was peeling one. Ashtray on the TV. In the kitchen, the oven had a steel handle, chipped, edge jutting like a blade. At first I thought there was a kid playing video games off the microwave, but my eyes adjusted: an old computer on the kitchen counter. Kid had to stand. He banged the mouse. He had a rat tail, knobby elbows. Maybe ten, eleven years-old? Game was three-dimensional, eye view. All you saw was a bazooka bobbing around. The kid made this bazooka kill some kind of lizard robot, then he made the bazooka run closer and take a few potshots at the corpse.

"You want some Baked Alaska?" Deseree asked. She was carrying a platter: ice cream, sponge cake, meringue. I was impressed. It's a tricky dish. Gotta throw it in the oven long enough to firm the meringue, but you can't forget all that ice cream. My wife, she always melts the ice cream. Deseree's looked perfect, stacks of browned foam, and I wanted some.

"Can't," I said. "Doctor's orders. Damn. That looks great."

Deseree smiled. "It's leftover from Ray's. I bake there."

"They say baking's a science and cooking's an art," Orrin said. He used a clementine peel to stir something in a mug. "But I say they need to shut up and have dessert at Deseree's."

Deseree put the Alaska in the refrigerator. On the kid's screen, the bazooka shot a crate, which exploded. Slime oozed down the walls, the same animation of slime down all the different walls. Then the bazooka shot some slime, but nothing happened. "Motherfucker," the kid said.

Deseree slapped his head. "Larkin," she said. "Watch your mouth."

"In Half Life you can shoot the slime," he said. "And then it melts, and then there's this hole, and then there's like this lair beneath the hole—"

Deseree crouched next to him and stared at the computer. "What is that, is that not Half Life?"

"It's like some stupid version," Larkin said. He banged the mouse. "Half Life for butt fags."

Deseree yanked the mouse from his hand and brandished it where he couldn't reach. "You say one more foulmouthed thing and I don't care what version that is, you're going to your room and you're reading a goddamn book."

"Sorry," he muttered. When she set down the mouse and walked away, I heard him mutter again, a stage whisper he wanted somebody to hear, I guess. "Not even my room" is what I heard. But my ears are old.

Deseree joined Orrin on the couch and smoked a cigarette. She blew rings at the ceiling. "The numbers is why they say that," she said. "About baking. They're right. You do the numbers and you're fine. There's no art."

"Art's in the eye of the ardent," Orrin said. He took a swig from his mug. He was enjoying himself. I sat on a recliner near the couch and Orrin tossed me a remote. "Something good," he said.

"Cable's out," Deseree said. She looked at the kid, then us. Made the money rub with her fingers. We nodded. She shrugged. "It's all lamebrains anyhow."

"Me and Brigham just did the opposite of TV," Orrin said. "Took ourselves a day-long redwood drive. Around 'em, through 'em, you name it."

Deseree shrugged again and leaned back, watching her smoke rise. "You talk to Ward lately?"

Orrin squinted into his mug. "What all you concocting in this tea—is that a starfish?"

"It's ginger root," Deseree said.

"Dessert With Deseree," he said. "It's a TV show waiting to happen."

"Ha. Thought you said this was the opposite of TV."

He pulled the root from the mug and bit it. "Did I? I wasn't listening."

Deseree got up and got the ashtray. She stood at the TV, tapping her cigarette. "We don't have much in the way of a guest room."

Orrin took another clementine. "We'll do a motel down the way."

Deseree looked at me. "You traveling with him now?"

I didn't know what she knew, so I was careful with my answer. "I live up in Crescent City. Right on the beach, pretty much."

Deseree snorted and nodded. "Well, I'm not much in the brain department myself. What the hell do I say to you guys?" She fluttered her cigarette at me. "I don't know how I precede myself, you know? Maybe I'm in a Christmas photo. Maybe you're like, who's that chick? Then Orrin here shits out the whole story. Or Wade. You close with your nephew, Brigham? You close with Captain Ward Hayworth?"

"Didn't know he was a captain," I said, which wasn't a lie.

"There we go," Deseree said. "Happy to share."

"He's not a captain," Orrin said. He sighed and picked at the clementine with his nail.

Then Larkin screamed, and I turned to see a giant tongue slurp out of a sand dune and slap the bazooka off-screen. Everything blanched red. White letters flashed: RESTART? RESTORE? Larkin started banging the mouse against the monitor. Deseree took a drag, slow, eyes shut, the tip of the cigarette orange and crinkling to ash. Then she snuffed the butt and walked to the computer, hit the power switch. Larkin whipped around, cussing like he was right off the poop deck, and tried to punch a dishtowel hanging on the oven handle.

His punch, of course, went through the towel. Steel sliced his knuckles. He howled. Deseree grabbed the towel and wrapped Larkin's hand.

I turned over the remote and saw the battery compartment open, empty. Wet carrots were what the trailer smelled like. If a carpet can look un-mown, that's how the carpet looked. Most people wouldn't cop to this, but I prefer boring. Boring is how I prefer my nights.

The towel went red.

Orrin creaked up. "You need anything?" he said.

"My hand's gonna die," Larkin said. His face was a garble of snot.

"Call something," Deseree said.

Orrin fumbled and dropped his cell phone. "Oh," he said.

I walked into the bathroom for rubbing alcohol, bandages, anything I could find. The shower curtain was black, covered in skulls and speech bubbles. GARY MARSHALL TATTOOS said the bubbles. Brigham, I asked myself, what the hell are you doing? Fishing through somebody else's medicine cabinet? Your credit's in good standing. Your porch doesn't leak. Typewriters wait for you to fix them then break again, just how you like. Satellites measure the wind chill in New Zealand and sprinkle the numbers into your weather inspector. Your wife, she puts a candle in the windowsill when she takes a bath, and that candle smells like butterscotch. If the instructions are good, you can make something do what's advertised in a cut-rate afternoon. Round about July, you forgo your shirt. Everything that's beautiful about Leigh and Gale is what makes them strange to you. Last time you saw Gale upset was on the phone, which isn't even seeing. Someone had stolen her social security number and you kept saying, "We'll get 'em, we'll catch 'em," but you couldn't hardly keep up, and your wife had to jump in and get efficient. Who decided the ocean should be so loud? It's none of your goddamn business, Brigham. Keep your life where you can hug it. That's the life you've earned. Come on, Brigham. Love is let live. Other people earn differently, which is not a thing to save them from.

"I found some cotton balls," I said. All three sat at that weird table, biographies and figurines shoved aside so Larkin could rest his towel-wrapped hand. Orrin was rigid, tapping rhythms. Deseree stroked Larkin's hair. He hiccuped and wiped his nose.

"Another night at the funny farm," Deseree said. "I'm sorry, guys."

What was funny was the three of us men types, wordless, each hearing for ourselves and taking what we assumed to be our share of that apology. "It's nothing," Orrin said. "We barged in."

I set the bag of cotton balls on the table next to a ceramic dragon.

Deseree petted Larkin's hair.

"It's an hour's drive," I said. "If we're being honest. Two tops. We can be home tonight."

Orrin stopped tapping. He squeezed the bag of cotton balls. His shirt was off by a button, and his cowlick was silver and goofed. Sure, those were his eyes, but they were somewhere else. Then is when Orrin cried.

It was shitty. What else can I say? Your big brother's there, his whole life, crying at some table—hell, you don't even know what room the table's in, or what to call who owns it. When we were kids, me and Orrin lived right on a bona fide cliff, near enough to the ocean that our house caught the arc of the Battery Point Lighthouse. In the pattern of that light is where I learned to sleep. What I'm trying to say is I've got my light and you've got yours. You can talk to your brother and he'll know what you mean, but the pattern's different for him. Even in the same bedroom. But there's a catch. When you bring a woman into your life, you get to ask what kind of light she's working off. And that's a hell of a thing. You get to ask. Then you both get to carry those separate lights together for a time, carry both lights all over, until you forget how your light started or where her light stops and everything seems close. Oh, maybe I shouldn't put it like that, Orrin. It's shitty. It doesn't all work out. You in a box and me in a suit. Orrin, we are gathered here to say it's shitty. You say my name, I'll say yours. But so long as we're here I hate to see you cry.

Deseree took Larkin into the bathroom. The gashes on his knuckles weren't all that deep. Me and Orrin sat awhile. I took off my glasses and set them on the table.

After a time, he looked up. "Portland's just up 5, right?"

"Rand McNally," I said. "He'd know better than me."

Orrin laughed, but laugh is the wrong word. "I'm good as gone, kiddo."

On the monitor, the game was still red, waiting on anybody, flashing options.

No Such Thing As a Wild Horse

So Jerry Friedstat owns the R/V Park plus the Family Fun Center. There's go-karts, bumper boats, and chili sauce not chili. Few years ago, his daughter got kidnapped. Right from the Fun Center. She was eating a churro, standing near the rowboat on the miniature golf course and staring at the freeway. Sometimes the SYSCO trucks spill and the drivers will say *shit* and sit down and eat the peaches with you, smile and close their eyes when you offer to help lie to their boss.

Well, Friedstat closed the Center for a year. Awkward as fuck when he would buy aspirin or shoe polish at the drugstore. You get what I mean. But then he started rebuilding. Went all out. Got this slick-ass cowboy theme. Everything a fake saloon or stable. Silver belly hats. I mean, he built this cross between a haunted house and shooting gallery. A mine shaft was the gimmick. You would clank through on a cart and shoot at these pop-up bats and cardboard banditos. He painted their mustaches neon so you could shoot their mustaches. Hella fun shit. Not to be all queer or anything, but I'd say Friedstat turned that Center from something rinky-dink into something grand. Something that was really something.

When you turn about thirteen, that's when you hear the story of the daughter. Right when you're really letting loose at the Center. Putt-putting or mashing the spray button on the boats, or I don't know—trying to sell them a lawnmower engine or whatever. That's pretty much when you hear about Friedstat's daughter.

Then, whenever they find a clump of bones in the woods near the quarry—and the papers tuck a write-up about the bones into the lower-left corner, right by the cartoon weather thing—you try to be the first one to talk about it. You go into Linda Riesling's Original Waffle House with the pictures of the flood from 1954, trying to spy out Linda's daughter, who listens to Rancid and fucks anything remotely hung. But it's only the VFW assholes and they say *you buy those pants from a nigger?* or *rub some alcohol on those zits, boy.* You try to sit down at the counter and order coffee, black. And you say *hey, did you hear about those bones? New bones. You think? I don't know. It's weird huh?*

And what they give you is hot chocolate, not coffee. Never coffee.

When I grow a beard, just a chinstrap maybe, and people believe me about things, I will say this: there is no such thing as a wild horse. The wild ones were made by God to buck the ghosts. That's pretty good, right? Maybe I should go to Nashville. But first I want to write that on a yellow Post-It note and leave it in the bathroom labeled Gents of Jerry Friedstat's joint. Then I will buy a corndog and I will steal somebody's R/V and I will drive and I will drive and I will drive until my bones come loose. Everything else—I'm sure—will feel like it does when you choke it.

ACKNOWLEDGMENTS

Here we go with that fat list that could spill forever and still fall short.

Dear friends in alphabetical order by first name: Adam Robinson, Alex (Maurice) Burford, Blake Butler, Bryan Coffelt, Chelsea Martin, Christopher Cheney, The Cinnamon Urns (past and present), David Rylance, Elliot and Erin Harmon, Gabe Durham, Jack Christian, Jordaan Mason, Kasey Mohammad, Kendra Grant Malone, Lindsay Rowan, Nat Otting, Patrick Duggan, Rachel B. Glaser, Ryan Call, and Wayne Lackey.

Mentors and editors in alphabetical order by last name: Chris Bachelder, Jedediah Berry, Elizabeth Ellen, Noy Holland, Jill Meyers, Sam Michel, Sabina Murray, Logan Ryan Smith, Dara Wier, Vincent Craig Wright, and especially, especialmente, Jackie Corley.

The supporters and amazing contributors to *NOÖ Journal* and Magic Helicopter Press.

Everyone else in the valleys Sacramento, Rogue, Pioneer, Zoetrope, and Independent Literature, who helped with these stories, let me sleep on their couch and eat their cereal, or just did their living thing with grace.

Mom, Dad, Holly, and Uncle Dave.

And finally: my carrot cake, my beautiful partner in coconut ice cream and openness, Carolyn Margaret Conspiracy Zaikowski.